FIGHT TO THE FINISH

Skye Fargo didn't mind a six-gun saloon show-down—except that the bartender had stripped him of his weapon and left him with only his bare fists. Still, he didn't mind a barroom brawl—except that in this case the man mountain called Big Jake was backed by six bruisers just as big.

Five savage minutes later, Fargo was on his back, with Big Jake looming over him. The heavy face was wavy as the pain swirled through Fargo. But Fargo felt a snapped table leg under his hand. He curled his fingers around it and thrust it upward, driving the splintered end into the snarling face. "Ow, goddamn," Big Jake swore as he staggered backward, streaming blood and curses. But the others leaped on Fargo as he tried to roll away.

One of them used the edge of a table to smash it into his ribs, and Fargo felt his flesh tear and the blood instantly soak his shirt. He knew the wave of weakness as it swept over him, and he realized they were going to kill him. . . .

**Be sure to read the other novels in
the exciting Trailsman series!**

THE
TRAILSMAN
176

CURSE
OF THE
GRIZZLY

by

Jon Sharpe

A SIGNET BOOK

SIGNET
Published by the Penguin Group
Penguin Books USA Inc., 375 Hudson Street,
New York, New York 10014, U.S.A.
Penguin Books Ltd, 27 Wrights Lane,
London W8 5TZ, England
Penguin Books Australia Ltd, Ringwood,
Victoria, Australia
Penguin Books Canada Ltd, 10 Alcorn Avenue,
Toronto, Ontario, Canada M4V 3B2
Penguin Books (N.Z.) Ltd, 182-190 Wairau Road,
Auckland 10, New Zealand

Penguin Books Ltd, Registered Offices:
Harmondsworth, Middlesex, England

First published by Signet, an imprint of Dutton Signet,
a division of Penguin Books USA Inc.

First Printing, August 1996
10 9 8 7 6 5 4 3 2

Copyright © Jon Sharpe, 1996
All rights reserved

The first chapter of this book originally appeared in *Betrayal at El Diablo*,
the one hundred seventy-fifth volume in this series.

 REGISTERED TRADEMARK—MARCA REGISTRADA

Printed in Canada

The Trailsman

Beginnings . . . they bend the tree and they mark the man. Skye Fargo was born when he was eighteen. Terror was his midwife, vengeance his first cry. Killing spawned Skye Fargo, ruthless, cold-blooded murder. Out of the acrid smoke of gunpowder still hanging in the air, he rose, cried out a promise never forgotten.

The Trailsman they began to call him all across the West: searcher, scout, hunter, the man who could see where others only looked, his skills for hire but not his soul, the man who lived each day to the fullest, yet trailed each tomorrow. Skye Fargo, the Trailsman, and the seeker who could take the wildness of a land and the wanting of a woman and make them his own.

*1860, northwest Colorado—
in the shadow of Pagoda Peak,
where a dark prophecy is played
out to its terrible finish . . . .*

1

Trouble.

Danger.

Signals.

All the silent, unspoken alarms.

The hair on the back of his neck grew stiff. The uneasiness stabbed at him, shapeless, having neither form nor meaning. Yet it was there, and the years had taught him not to ignore the messages that came on silent, unseen wings. He had spent a lifetime learning to read the signs that came from outside, the mark on a lead, the trail in the blade of grass, the turn of a bush, and the crumbled pattern of the soil. He knew the way of men and of all the creatures that walked, flew, or crawled. He understood the messages in their every step, their every flurry of wings, the alarms in their every cry and call.

He was the Trailsman, a part of the sounds and the ways of all nature and all the things of nature. He knew all he could see, smell, hear, taste, touch, but he also knew the power of those things that defied explanation, those messages that came from beyond the senses. Skye Fargo's lake blue eyes scoured the terrain as he ran one hand along the Ovaro's jet black neck. The horse had been the first to pick up trouble, as it so often did, and Fargo had absolute trust in the reliability of sensitivities beyond his own. The Ovaro's ears had been the first sign, suddenly moving back and forth, tilting forward, then flattening, then twitching to one side or the other. Then he felt the faint but unmistakable tension in the horse's black-and-white body and finally the short tattoo of hooves instead of the usual smooth stride.

Fargo let his eyes scan the land again, but there was nothing save the lush foliage of golden aspen and hackberry. The north Colorado territory was a rich land, ripe with foliage, flat with deep grasses, and mountainous with the northern conifers. Game abounded in this land—elk, bighorn sheep, cougar, fox, wolf, bear, and all the smaller creatures. But he saw nothing to give him alarm, yet the horse still beat a nervous tattoo with its hooves. Fargo steered the horse under the wide branches of a hackberry and swung to the ground. He let the horse calm itself in the shade of the big tree and continued to rub his hand soothingly against the warm fur. His eyes narrowing as they again traversed the terrain, Fargo heard the soft curse escape his lips and grew angry with himself.

Stupid. Ridiculous. He bit the words out silently as he swore at himself. Yet the moment had flung itself at him out of yesterdays, words he had scoffed at then suddenly whirling at him with a malicious fury all their own. They rose out of a moment three weeks back in the Oklahoma territory. He let a wry smile edge his lips. It had not been a completely bad experience. In fact, most of it had been damn nice, but it hadn't been the nice part that had suddenly leaped at him from out of the blue. He saw that the horse had calmed down, and he lowered himself to the ground and leaned back against the bumpy, gray bark of an old hackberry. He half closed his eyes and turned the days backward in his mind. Not that he had much choice, for they continued to stay with him, demanding to be relived again.

Part of it had been his own fault, the result of too much bourbon, too much money in his pocket, and too much of a warm, willing woman. It was a combination he had never been able to resist, and he saw no reason to do so then. The bourbon had been a reward to himself for a very long, very hot trail drive all the way up from Houston, filled with unexpected problems. The extra money was the kind of advance on a new job no reasonable man could turn down. The little town in the Oklahoma territory had a name, Stillwater, and he'd enjoyed the evening relaxing at the Stillwater Saloon as he looked forward to the room and bed he'd taken at the town inn. It was near midnight when he finished the last drink and walked the nearly deserted street toward the inn.

That's when he met her, standing beside the wagon, trying to close a tailgate that refused to close. He took in the wagon for a moment and saw it was an Owensboro Texas wagon outfitted with bows for a canvas top, big and bulky with the driver's seat under the canvas top. The wheels wore extra wide steel rims, he noted, one in the left rear bearing the ridged mark of a collision with a sharp rock. He turned back to the young woman to stare at lush, simmering beauty. Long, thick black hair fell almost to the middle of her back, framing deep brown, liquid eyes with thick, black brows that matched her hair. The liquid eyes, slightly almond-shaped, looked at him from out of an olive-skinned face with an aquiline nose and full lips that virtually quivered with sensuality. A scoop-necked, white peasant blouse revealed the deep cleavage of full breasts, and a black skirt covered womanly hips. Fargo saw the liquid eyes slowly move across the chiseled planes of his face.

He took a step forward, curled one hand around the top edge of the recalcitrant gate, and, using his powerful shoulder muscles, pushed it closed. The hint of a smile touched the young woman's full lips. "Thank you. A handsome rescuer, a very handsome one. Thank you, again," she said. He immediately heard the accent in her speech, not one he could recognize.

"My pleasure. Don't usually get to help someone so damn beautiful," Fargo said.

Her smile was slow and simmering. "What do they call you, handsome man?" she asked, the faint accent intriguing.

"Fargo . . . Skye Fargo," he said. "And you?"

"Irina," she said.

"Never heard that name before. Where are you from?" Fargo asked.

"Hungary," she said, and Fargo nodded as he let his eyes go back to the Owensboro with its makeshift canvas top. Strange markings were painted onto the canvas, the outline of an eye, a triangle inside a circle, a crudely drawn hand holding a glowing candle between the third and fourth fingers, a cross standing upside down, and words he couldn't understand. "You have not seen our wagon before?" Irina asked.

"No," Fargo answered. "*Our* wagon?"

"It belongs to my brother and me," she said and had just finished the sentence when Fargo saw the figure trudging toward the wagon with a bucket of water. The man paused at the front of the wagon, a dark, brooding face on a stolid, slightly hunched body. "Mikhail," Irina said. The man grunted and stepped into the wagon with the bucket.

"He always so friendly?" Fargo commented.

"We have come a long way. It has been hard for him," she said.

"A long way from where?" Fargo asked.

"Hungary," Irina said. "We are Gypsies. Our family have been Gypsies for hundreds of years."

"How'd you wind up here?" Fargo frowned.

"A rich man paid me to tell his fortune, to read the cards for him every day, to give him the ancient wisdom of the Gypsies. He brought us here, and then he died. I told him he would," she said with a diffident shrug.

"And now?"

"I try to earn enough to go home someday. I tell fortunes. I read the cards," she said.

"The cards?"

"The tarot cards," she said.

"That all?" he questioned.

Her half-smile widened. "A girl must live, earn her way," she said and came closer, her deep breasts almost touching his chest, a faintly musky odor to her, strangely exciting. "For you, my handsome friend, I would give myself. You are too handsome to ask anything more. But Mikhail would be very angry, very angry," she said.

"Angry enough to beat you?" Fargo asked.

"It's happened," Irina said. "He knows no other ways. Nobody will give him work here."

Fargo's hand slipped around the back of her neck. Her skin was warm and smooth under the thick, black hair, the musky odor of her again exciting. She was entirely too much woman to pass up. "I'm at the inn, room three," he said.

She nodded, and there was real heat in the liquid eyes. "I will tell your fortune, too," she said, and he pulled his hand away and walked on with a quick glance back at the Gypsy wagon. Irina had disappeared inside, and he hurried away. At the inn he undressed down to his undershorts and let a deep sigh of contentment escape as he stretched out on the luxury that was a bed. The Ovaro was in the stable, fed, groomed, and enjoying its own brand of comfort. They had both earned it, Fargo murmured silently.

The knock at the door was not long in coming, a soft yet firm sound. "It's open," he said, and she entered, halting at the side of the bed, liquid eyes taking in the smoothly muscled contours of his torso.

"The most handsome man I have seen in this big country," she said.

"I'm not going to disagree," Fargo said as Irina reached into her skirt pocket and brought out a small, stoppered bottle, two small clay cups each hardly larger than a shot glass, and a deck of cards.

Egri Bikaver, wine from Hungary, for later, when I read the cards for you," she said, putting everything on top of the battered bureau against one wall. Her fingers, long and slender, were unbuttoning the white blouse as she returned to the bed. She pulled the blouse from her, and Fargo stared at the two full, deep, olive-skinned mounds, smooth and voluptuous, each tipped with a dark pink circle and in the center of each areola, a firm, red nipple. She undid the black skirt, it fell to the floor, and she stepped out of dark bloomers to stand before him, a throbbingly beautiful figure, deep breasts swaying slightly, round barrel chest beneath, and full, wide hips with a rounded belly that fit the rest of her lush body. A thick, inky triangle of unkempt hair stood out in perfect accompaniment to her, and just below, full-flashed thighs that might someday be heavy, but were now only beautifully ripe.

His arms reached out, and she came down half atop him, the full lips on his, encompassing, working, sucking, and he felt her tongue reach out at once, wet caresses, harbinger thrustings, and the deep breasts were surprisingly firm pillows against his chest. His mouth found one, drew in the red nipple, and pulled on it. Irina uttered a deep, growling sigh, and felt her hands crawl down his body, across his groin, and find his burgeoning organ. "Ah, good, yes, yes, aaaaaah . . ." she breathed as she stroked and pressed and drew her thighs upward. Her deep, thick triangle pressed against his groin, little soft-wire strands moving against his legs.

"Ah, good, is good, is good," Irina cried out as he let his hand find her wet warmth, and she almost threw herself onto her back, the full-fleshed thighs opening for him as he touched, and caressed, then reached into her silky tunnel. Irina's belly rose up, and slapped against his groin, growling gasps coming from her as she reached for him, closed her fingers around him, and pulled him to her. "Yes, yes, yes, please, good, oh, good," Irina cried out, and her musky odor was stronger, stimulating, an erotic perfume of the woman wanting without reserve. This was no performance, no charade of motion, but a body erupting in all its honest passion, and when he slid forward into her dark wetness, her breasts rose up, and she thrust forward, her hands pulling his head down to the olive-skinned mounds. Deep, growling gasps continued to come from her as she rose and fell with him, flesh urging flesh, passion feeding on passion, the spiral reaching upward, her fleshy thighs quivering around his hips as though they would never fall away.

Her cry remained a kind of growl even as it rose in pitch. "Ah, my God, aaaggggh . . . I come, I come for you, oh, handsome man, I come for you," Irina half screamed, and she came, and came again, and again, crying and bucking, smothering his head in the deep breasts until he wondered if she'd ever stop. But she did, finally, with a growling, guttural cry, and sank down with him, clasped against him with all of her lush body. When her arms relaxed from around him and her thighs dropped from around his waist, she uttered another deep sigh. Finally, she pushed onto one elbow, then sat up, and the deep mounds swayed together as she met his stare, liquid eyes still swimming with their dark depths.

"Are all Gypsy girls like you?" he asked.

She gave a half-shrug. "Gypsies do not hold back. Passion is in our blood," she said. "Sometimes it is wasted. But with you it was all worth it."

"Take whatever you want from my jacket pocket," he said.

"Later. We do not need to talk of such now, not with you," Irina said, then swung herself from the bed. He watched her ample rear move as she walked to the bureau. She opened the little bottle and filled the two small cups, returned, and handed him one as she sat on the edge of the bed. She raised her cup and drank it down in one gulp as he did his, the wine a full-bodied dark red, sweet yet not cloying. She took the emptied cups back to the bureau and returned with the deck of cards to sit cross-legged on the bed as she spread the cards on the sheet, and her lush nakedness seemed absolutely natural.

His eyes went to the cards she spread, then shuffled together, and he saw drawings on each, some that seemed witches, others naked women or fiery objects, and he noted four suits, one of swords, another wands, one of grails, and the last of pentacles. She mixed the cards again and put the deck in front of him. "Touch the cards. How you say, cut the deck," she said. He picked up the tarot cards, cut the deck, and handed them back to her. "That important?" he asked.

"Very. I read the cards for you. Now you have touched them, you have put yourself inside them. It makes it all stronger," she said and leaned forward as she shuffled through the cards, suddenly intensely studying the cards as she turned up one after another. Her full breasts hung forward, almost touching the cards, and he happily enjoyed the beauty of her. Suddenly, she stopped and sat up straight, and he saw the deep, liquid eyes turn even darker as she stared at him. "It is bad, very bad. The cards say it, they say you will be killed," she said, and he saw the furrow creasing her smooth brow.

Fargo allowed a half-smile. "They tell you when?" he asked casually.

"No, they do not say that," she answered.

"They tell you how?" he pressed, tolerance in his voice.

"Yes," she said, scanning the cards again and then looking back at him. "There will be a terrible battle. You will be torn apart, ripped to little pieces."

"Well, now, people have said I was going to be killed a lot of times, and they were always wrong." Fargo smiled.

"You do not believe the cards. That is bad. They never lie," Irina said, her voice growing agitated. She took the cards and pulled them together back into a deck, uncrossed her legs, and swept her skirt up, stepping into it quickly. The white blouse came next, and he saw the anger and concern in her face.

"Now, calm down," Fargo said evenly and started to reach out for her when suddenly Irina became two persons, separating in front of him. He halted and shook his head, and she swam back to one person. Fargo reached out again and felt the wave of dizziness sweep over him. He shook his head and saw Irina almost fade from his vision. "Goddamn," he gasped, trying to move toward her, his legs suddenly made of lead. He felt himself falling forward to the end of the bed, and he shook away a gray curtain that had descended before his eyes. Irina came clear for a moment, watching him, and then the curtain descended again. His head fell forward to the foot of the bed. "Goddamn," he heard himself muttering. "Goddamn." He felt the bedsheet against his face, but only for another moment, and then the world disappeared. "Bitch," Fargo murmured, but knew he was the only one who heard the word, and then there was nothing more.

2

His eyelids fluttered. It was the first sign and he lay still as time remained suspended. Finally, he opened his eyes and let the curtain of grayness slowly lift. The lone window of the room took shape, the stream of sunlight shafting through it. The rest of the room materialized, and Fargo slowly pushed himself onto his forearms, turned, and winced at the throbbing inside his head. Moving slowly, he sat up, waited, and let the last of the drug drift from him as he softly cursed. The night swam back over him, and his curses grew louder. He swung long legs over the edge of the bed, suddenly aware of his nakedness, and started to pull on trousers, then boots. The shirt came next, and when he took his jacket, he found all his money was gone. That was no surprise.

He looked to where he'd put his saddle in a corner of the room. The saddle was still there, but he saw that the rifle case was empty, the big Henry missing from it. His eyes snapped to where his holster hung over the back of the chair. It, too, hung empty, the Colt gone. "Of course, goddammit," Fargo hissed bitterly. Both guns would fetch a handsome price. He finished dressing, his head still throbbing, and left the inn, glad he'd paid for his room in advance. When he reached the stable, the throbbing in his head had begun to diminish. He saddled his horse and rode from the stable, every moment of the night now all too clear in his mind. Gypsies, he spat out silently. The simmering Irina had been good, very good, using her sensuous beauty as a mask for her thievery.

He hadn't suspected a thing, he admitted with some chagrin. Perhaps, if she hadn't drunk the wine from the very same bottle, he might have grown wary. But she had, and the fact still stuck inside him. The answer, of course, was as simple as it was clever. The cup she'd given him had the knockout powder already inside, coating the bottom, impossible to taste in the sweetness of the wine. Everything smoothly planned and equally smoothly performed. Damn, Fargo swore as he pulled the Ovaro to a halt where he'd first met Irina beside the wagon. The ground was laid over with new wagon tracks as well as hoofprints.

The average man would never have found the wagon tracks, which the Gypsies counted on, of course. However, he wasn't the average man. He had noticed more about the wagon than others would have seen, and now his trailsman's experience let his gaze sweep the ground with a special knowledge, seeking out the set of tracks he had to separate from the others. It didn't take all that long before he picked out the extra-wide wheel imprints with the cut in the left rear steel tire. He turned the Ovaro and sent the horse after the marks at a slow trot. They had gone north from town into gently rolling hills where the trail grew sharper as the other tracks disappeared. He found where they had halted to camp, dismounted, and let the soil pass through his fingers as he tested the rate at which it crumbled at his touch. They had been there some four hours earlier, he estimated, and he increased the pinto's pace.

The land grew thicker with a long stand of box elder and high brush, but the tracks followed a narrow road that cut through the forest. Fargo sent the pinto over a low rise that let him look down at the road and reined to a halt a few thousand yards ahead. The Owensboro stood in a small leafy alcove. He slid from the horse and moved forward on foot, and he saw the movement at the rear of the wagon. It took shape, became Mikhail, his stolid figure carrying an armful of laundry. Fargo stayed in the box elder and circled closer where the trees halted less than a dozen feet from the wagon. Mikhail was the only one visible, and Fargo moved quickly on silent steps, darting from the trees in a half crouch.

The man felt his presence and spun just as Fargo's fist smashed into his jaw, and he went down in an explosion of laundry. Fargo stepped over him to the rear of the wagon, pulled the canvas back, and Irina looked up from the cluttered interior of the wagon. He reached in, grabbed her arm, and yanked. She came flying out of the wagon and went sprawling on the ground, the deep, liquid eyes staring up at him in astonishment. "Bitch," he said, peering back inside the jumbled wagon. He spotted the rifle propped up against one side and pulled it out, turned, and saw Irina had pushed to her feet, the deep eyes frowning at him. Being a damn thief didn't make her any less beautiful, he noted.

"How did you find us?" she asked.

"Gypsies make mistakes," he said.

"Luck?"

"No. You read cards. I read trails," he said. "But you were good, I'll give you that much." She shrugged, the gesture more defiant than contrite. "I'll take the money," he said, and she didn't move. "Or I'll wring your lying, thieving little neck," he said. He took a step closer to her. "You made one mistake about me. Don't make another," he growled. She reached into her skirt pocket and drew out the roll of bills, glowering at him as she did. "You'll forgive me if I don't say thanks," Fargo tossed at her as he took the money. He'd just put the bills in his pocket when he caught the sound from behind him.

He whirled, the rifle in his hands, to see Mikhail charging, a long-handled axe upraised. Fargo twisted away as he ducked and felt the axe graze the top of his head. He thrust the barrel of the rifle forward, ramming it straight into the man's abdomen. Mikhail let out a sharp gasp of pain as he doubled over, and Fargo brought the butt of the rifle up and around. It smashed into Mikhail's temple, and he went down, unconscious before he hit the ground. Fargo spun again to see Irina leaping into the wagon. She was already inside when he caught her as she tried to pull the Colt from under a pillow. He spun her around, knocked the pistol from her hand, and flung her out of the wagon.

He followed, holstering the Colt as Irina climbed back to her feet. "You're lucky," he said. "I don't have time to track down a sheriff and have you jailed. Chances are you'd be out and back in business in a few weeks, anyway." Uttering a contemptuous grunt, he glanced at her brother, who was still unconscious, and turned back to her. "Shove it, honey, you and your crazy cards."

"No!" Irina screamed, and he saw her eyes grow wide, and then her hands were against his chest, curling into his shirt. "The tarot cards are not crazy. The cards do not lie. I read what they say. It will all come true," she said, her

liquid eyes boring into him. He pulled her hands from his shirt, backed away, and swung onto the pinto as she stared after him. "The cards do not lie. You wait and see," she shouted. She was still screaming after him as he rode away, shaking his head with a mixture of amazement and disdain. Gypsy ways were beyond his understanding, he decided.

The days stopped unreeling. Yesterdays became today, and Fargo felt the warty bark of the old hackberry against his back. But the furrow stayed on his brow as he pushed to his feet. He had laughed away the Gypsy girl's threat and dismissed her tarot cards as so much empty fakery. Yet now they had flung themselves at him, rising out of other days with a strange vengeance. The mind plays its own tricks, he murmured as he once again dismissed all of it, impatience, even annoyance pushing at him. He swung onto the Ovaro and sent the horse north through the rich countryside. But it didn't take more than another five minutes for the Ovaro to tense again.

This time Fargo kept the horse moving forward, but he brought the reins in tight, let his legs press firmly into the horse's ribs, and used his body to transmit assurance. The horse tried to respond and fought against its nervousness, and Fargo stroked the massive, jet black neck as he rode across a slope thickly covered with goosegrass and two-foot-tall patches of broomsedge. The house came into sight some thousand feet ahead, an old wood frame structure, and next to it a sagging barn with peeling paint. Fargo steered the horse toward the structure and was perhaps halfway to it when the Ovaro halted, stepped backward, and tossed its head. Fargo glimpsed something in the tall broomsedge patch just ahead, swung from the saddle, and let the horse stay back as he walked to the object.

"Jesus," he heard himself gasp as he stared down at the lower part of a man's leg. It had been torn off at the knee, the blood very red and fresh, running down over the calf. He stared at it, his lake blue eyes narrowed, then lifted his gaze to the land that stretched out in front of him. His hand had dropped to rest on the Colt, an automatic reflex. Straightening, he took the pinto by the reins and walked forward again toward the house and barn. He'd gone another few hundred feet, the horse pulling back, going with him reluctantly, when he saw another object in the grass. He heard the oath fall from his lips again as he found himself staring down at the upper half of a man's leg.

He saw the thigh exposed, the flesh stripped off the hip down to what was left of his knee. There were other marks, deep gouges of flesh ripped away and torn sections of the upper thigh. Fargo pushed to his feet and walked on, pulling the pinto behind him. The tracks took form on the ground, huge and unmistakable, and he had almost reached the house when he found the mangled torso, the ribs caved in, a huge piece of the chest eaten away. Fargo studied the grisly sight as his hand stayed on the butt of the Colt. When he looked away, he considered taking the rifle from its saddle case, aware that a pistol would be useless unless it hit the exact right spot.

He heard the moan and spun, then followed the sound to the barn where he saw the figure lying facedown, halfway out the barn door. He knelt down and saw dark blond hair worn in a ponytail, the soft cheek of a young woman clothed in a dark red shirt. She stirred, moaned again, her eyes opening as she pushed up on her hands.

He helped her sit up and saw a small nose, a pert face, pretty in a fresh, scrubbed way. She blinked at him, regaining consciousness, and he saw soft, mist blue eyes and smallish breasts pressing against the shirt. "You hit me?" she questioned.

"No. I was riding by," Fargo said.

"Somebody hit me as I came out of the barn," she said, suspicion in her face. He leaned over and looked at the back of her head just over the ponytail. A welt had risen under a small abrasion in her scalp.

"So they did," Fargo grunted. "But it wasn't me." He helped her to her feet as her pretty face screwed up in a wince.

"I've got to see if Amos is all right," she said and started to walk away. He held an arm out and stopped her.

"Who's Amos?" he asked.

"My uncle, Amos Cool. I live here with him," she said.

Fargo kept his face expressionless as the picture of the mangled torso flashed through his mind. "He wear a blue checked shirt?" Fargo asked.

She frowned at once. "His favorite. Why?" Without waiting for an answer, she started to push past, but Fargo's arm held her back.

"You don't want to go out there," he said.

Her mist blue eyes darkened, and then she darted around him, raced down the grass, and Fargo swore softly as he saw her come to a halt and stare down at the grass. Her scream came, pierced the air, a terrible, shattering cry that reverberated through the trees nearby. He ran to where she stood with hands clasped to her face, took her by the arm, and pulled her away. "Oh, my God,

25

my God, my God," the young woman repeated almost numbly. He led her away toward the house, where she halted and fell against him, her face white with shock. "He's been torn apart. What did this? A cougar?" she asked.

"Did you hear anything?" Fargo asked.

"I was in the barn, and I heard a noise. I thought it was Amos's voice. I started to come out. That's when I was hit on the head. I thought it was somebody hiding outside," she said. "But it had to have been whatever attacked Amos. Was it a cougar? God, he was ripped apart."

"No cougar," Fargo said.

"Then what? I've never seen wolves do this, not even a pack, not so fast," she said.

"No wolves," Fargo said, seeing the carnage in his mind, seeing the lower leg torn off at the knee, the flesh ripped down the upper thigh.

"Then what?" the young woman asked as she sank to the ground, shock wreathing her face. He knelt down beside her on one knee.

"Grizzly. Only a giant grizzly could have done this, crushed his chest in with one bite," Fargo said. "A real giant of a grizzly."

"The Carrigans said they had seen a huge grizzly around their place," she said.

"Where's that?"

"Not far, down in the hollow. They've got two kids," she said. She touched the top of her head gingerly. "Then it was the grizzly that hit me," she said.

"No," Fargo said with a wry grunt. "A grizzly would have smashed your head in and left huge claw marks."

"You saying someone hit me?"

"Looks that way. Whoever did it saved your life," Fargo said, and she frowned her question. "You were left unconscious. A grizzly won't usually bother someone unconscious."

She put her hands to her face and rocked back and forth. "Oh, God, oh, God," she murmured.

"Why would someone hit you?" Fargo questioned.

"That's a long story," she said and pushed to her feet, biting her lips together. "I've got to see to Amos," she said.

"No, you don't," he said. "That'll be too damn hard for you. I'll see to that. But first you've got to get your head looked at. There a doc anywhere around here?"

"Yes, in Hobsonville, a couple miles down valley," she said. "It's not much of a town, a few buildings, the saloon, and Doc Peterson."

"I'll take you. I don't think you're up to riding on your own," Fargo said.

"Thanks." She nodded. "I'm still kind of dizzy, and my stomach feels like it's all twisted together." She let his hand help her onto the Ovaro, and he swung onto the horse behind her where she sat back, a very soft rear pressed against his groin. She kept her eyes closed as he steered the pinto past the torn remains that dotted the ground and opened them only after they'd gone a few hundred yards. "Go down the slope and turn right," she said. "What's your name, mister?"

"Skye Fargo," he said.

"I'm Toby Denison," she said. "I'm obliged for your kindness. How come you know so much about what killed Amos?"

"They call me the Trailsman, and that means knowing everything there is to know about signs," he said, and she turned her head to look back at him, a tiny furrow creasing her brow as she studied him. It was an appraising look, and it seemed as though she were going to say something more, but she didn't and faced the front of the horse again. Fargo found the bottom of the slope and turned the horse along a narrow road almost grown over with vervain and a line of Rocky Mountain maple alongside. "What'd you and Amos do out here?" he asked.

"Amos did leatherwork. He was a real craftsman. He could do wonderful things with leather—bags, belts, clothes, boots. I was his helper, his apprentice," she said. "People heard about his work. They'd come, put in orders, and twice a year we'd go to Medicine Bow up in Wyoming."

Fargo spied a distant house and barn and a corral of hogs as he rode along the half-valley. "A lot of small ranchers around here?" he asked.

"A few, a new family every year or so," Toby Denison said. "Mostly around here we've out-of-work cowhands, old prospectors still looking for a strike, a few sheep ranches, and a lot of drifters."

He caught the contempt in her voice. "Sounds as though you're not too happy here," he remarked.

"Amos was the only thing worthwhile," she said, the sob catching in her voice at once.

"You been with him long?" he questioned.

"Four years, since my ma died back in New Mexico," the girl said.

"You want to tell me why somebody hit you on the head?" he asked.

"No," she said firmly.

"They still did you a favor, unintentionally," Fargo said.

"I'll remember to thank them," she said, bitterness in her voice. She was a lot more grown-up than the youthfulness in her face indicated, and harder than the mist blue eyes offered. The small half-valley came to an end, and Fargo saw the small knot of buildings rise up in front of him. "Hobsonville," Toby said. "The doc's place is at the end of town." He steered the horse down the single main street. She hadn't exaggerated the ordinariness of the town, yet the street was busy enough with foot and horse traffic, and he saw a half-dozen farm wagons and a few two-horse seedbed rigs. At Toby's direction he drew up before a small, neat white house and she slid to the ground.

He followed her inside where Doc Peterson turned out to be younger than he'd expected, a tall figure with curly brown hair, spectacles, and a serious manner. As the doctor examined Toby's head, Fargo told him about Amos Cool and the grizzly. "Good God," Doc Peterson said. "Poor Toby. You see it?"

"No," Toby said.

"I'll get Sam Tilton soon as I finish. Sam does all our burying work around here," the doctor explained to Fargo. "You think Amos stumbled onto a she-bear with cubs?" he asked.

"No. I saw only one set of tracks, goddamn big tracks," Fargo said.

"Never heard of a grizzly just up and tearing somebody apart like that," the doctor said.

"It happens. A bear turns rogue, usually an older bear. He finds out how easy it is to bring down a human, develops a taste for it, and becomes a real killer. I'm afraid that's what you have here. There's not much more dangerous than a rogue grizzly."

"I'll spread the word on my rounds," the doctor said. "How'd you hurt your head, Toby?"

"I fell," the girl said and ignored Fargo's surprised glance at her. When the doctor stepped into an adjoining room, Fargo leaned forward to her.

"You lie to me, or are you lying to him?" he asked.

"To him. I don't want a lot of questions," she half whispered. She turned the mist blue eyes on him, a kind of defiance in their veiled depths.

"Not much of an answer," he said.

"Enough for now," she said.

"I'd think about going back to your place for now," Fargo said. "Maybe I ought to go back with you."

"You're on your way to the Farrell place," Toby Denison said, and Fargo's brow furrowed at once.

"How'd you know that?" he asked in surprise.

"Word's out," she said.

"You want to tell me what word?" he asked, frowning.

"No," she said, and the doctor returned with a small bandage for the top of her head.

"I've a feeling I'll be seeing you again, Toby Denison," Fargo said as he started for the door.

She gave a half-shrug, and Doc Peterson nodded to him. "I'll see to Sam Tilton. I won't let her go back till things are cleared away," he said.

"That'd be best," Fargo said from the doorway.

"I decide what I do," Toby Denison said.

"Make it hard as you like on yourself. Your call," Fargo thrusted at her, and she tossed him a half-glower as she took a deep swallow. She didn't answer, but he saw the tears edging her eyes. He walked from the house and climbed onto the Ovaro when she stepped from the doorway, hands in the pockets of her skirt.

"Go north from my place," she said truculently.

"Thanks," he said and put the horse into a trot. A young woman as prickly as she was pretty. Perhaps it was just reaction to the shock of what had happened, but there was more, he felt certain, and he rode back to her house and slowed to look again at the mangled torso. There'd be other parts near, he knew, but he had no desire to find them, and he rode on, staying north along a series of gently rolling hills until he reached a drop in the land where a low-roofed house appeared, a barn behind it, and he drew to a halt outside a stone front built below wooden structure. Two men stepped from the house, both hard-eyed, scanning him suspiciously.

"Looking for Stu Farrell," Fargo said.

"Who might you be?" one asked from under a small, bristly mustache.

"Name's Fargo . . . Sky Fargo," the Trailsman said and saw the two men exchange quick glances.

"This way, mister," the mustached one said, and Fargo slid from the Ovaro and followed the men into a large room with heavy, solid furniture, quilted rugs on the floor, and Indian blankets on the walls. Two doorways led off to other rooms. "He's here," the one man called out, and moments later a figure stepped through the doorway—tall, willowy, black hair cut short, clothed in a tan, one-piece outfit that emphasized the outline of narrow hips, wide shoulders, and long breasts. He took in sharp, dark brown eyes, straight nose and wide mouth, and a very attractive face of some thirty years, he guessed.

"Hello," she said, her voice clear, instant authority in just the one word. "I'm Elise Farrell. I'm the one that sent you the note and the advance."

Fargo frowned. "It was signed Stuart Farrell," he said.

"My late husband," Elise Farrell said. "Some men don't like to work for a woman. I thought I'd take no chances."

"Money's money," Fargo said.

"Please, sit down," Elise Farrell said, and her smile softened the authority of her tone. She gestured to the mustached man. "This is Rick Chowder," she said. "And Ernie Walters. They're two of my four guards."

"Guards?" Fargo said as he sat down on the edge of a buckskin-covered sofa.

"Guards, helpers, all-around hands," Elise Farrell said, and at a curt nod from her both men walked from the room.

"How long have you been here alone?" Fargo asked, and Elise Farrell sat down beside him. She moved with easy grace, longish breasts swaying slightly.

"Three months," she said.

"Your husband have an accident?" Fargo frowned.

"No. Stuart was past seventy," Elise Farrell said and smiled as Fargo's brows lifted. "He wanted a young wife, if just to admire. He died quickly, suddenly."

"Sorry about that," Fargo said. "You spent your years with him being admired, I'd guess."

"Yes," Elise Farrell said. "You disapprove?"

"Hell, no. But it wouldn't be enough for some women," Fargo remarked.

"I didn't say it was enough. One learns to make do," she said coolly. "But I didn't bring you out here to talk about my life." He heard the authority quickly return to her voice.

"I'm just naturally curious," Fargo said. "Your letter said something about a map and a silver mine."

"That's right. I hired you to follow the map and find the mine," she said.

"I'm a little confused. If you've a map, why don't you just follow it? What do you need me for?" Fargo questioned.

"It will be a very loosely drawn map, hardly a map at all," she said, and the frown returned to Fargo's brow.

"Will be?" he asked.

Elise Farrell looked uncomfortable suddenly. "I thought I'd have the map by now, but I don't," she said. "We've really been looking for it. Unfortunately, we haven't found it."

"Maybe you'd best start at the beginning," Fargo said, and Elise nodded and settled back, her willowy figure graceful against the sofa.

"Stuart Farrell made a lot of money silver mining during his lifetime. He lived well and gambled away most of it. But he always said he'd save one mine, a secret, rich vein, to give someone when he died. He said he'd made a map of how to find the mine, but he always laughed when he used the word *map*. I know Stuart. It'll be a collection of loose notes, obscure directions, and cryptic marks. That's why I hired you. I'll need you to decipher it, make it real, and find the mine." She halted, her eyes watching him sharply.

"Why'd you take on four guards?" Fargo questioned.

"Stuart talked too much about his hidden mine. There are a lot of people who'd like to find the map. They don't know it wouldn't do them much good," Elise Farrell said. "I'm sure there are people who'd kill for it."

"All of which means I wait around until you find the map, or whatever," Fargo said.

"No. Now that you're here, you can help look for the map. I'll tell you everything I know about Stuart's habits. Maybe you'll come up with something," the woman said.

"I can't see myself coming up with any place you haven't looked," Fargo said.

"You'll bring a fresh perspective," Elise said, and her hand reached out and covered his. "Work with me on this. You won't regret it. I can be very grateful."

"That's nice," Fargo said, and she squeezed his hand a moment longer, then drew back at a sound from the doorway. He looked up to see Toby Denison enter. Elise Farrell stood up at once, her face tightening.

"What are you doing here?" she asked the younger woman.

"Come to see him," Toby said, and the room suddenly crackled with tension.

"What for, and how'd you know he was here?" Elise Farrell snapped.

Fargo spoke up, interrupting the exchange. "We met, not under the best of circumstances," he said.

"Amos was killed," Toby said, her voice flat.

"Torn apart, a grizzly," Fargo said. Elise's eyes widened, but he saw no sympathy in them, no shocked concern, only surprise.

"Jesus," she said.

"Fargo found him," Toby volunteered.

"So what brings you here?" Elise Farrell questioned, the edge back in her voice.

"He said he'd go back with me. I'm here to take him up on it," Toby said with a long glance at Fargo.

"Wait outside," Elise said to her, curtly and coldly. Toby walked from the room, tossing a disdainful glance back at the older woman. Elise turned to Fargo. "Forget about her. She can go back on her own," the woman said.

"She can get herself killed doing that," Fargo said.

"That's not my problem. It's not yours, either. You're working for me. I want you here," Elise Farrell said bitingly, ice in her tone.

"Whoa, there, honey," Fargo said. "You're not even ready for me. You don't need me yet. She does."

"You expect to baby-sit her forever? That grizzly could come back anytime," Elise said.

"True enough, but chances are he'll come nosing around tonight. It'd fit grizzly behavior. If I can scare him off, it might be enough to send him away to find other places. The least I can do is give her some advice on protecting herself," Fargo said.

"And if he comes back tonight, he could get you. I can't risk that. You'll stay here," Elise said, and Fargo felt irritation at her icy imperiousness.

"I'll be taking her back," he said quietly. "I think a life's more important than searching for a map, which you can do on your own."

"I've my interests to think about," she said.

"And I want to be able to look in the mirror every morning," Fargo said, rising to his feet.

"I expect people who work for me to obey my orders," she said, her fine features tight with anger.

"I don't work for you, honey. You paid me to come do a job for you. That doesn't make me a hired hand," he said.

"You walk out of here, and you can stay out," Elise Farrell hissed.

"Your call," Fargo said. As he brushed past her, he detected the faint aroma of violet, the scent both pristine and provocative. Entirely in keeping with Elise Farrell, he decided.

"Go to hell, Fargo," her voice called after him as he walked to the Ovaro. Toby Denison waited on a light brown mare.

"Ride," he growled and put the pinto into a trot.

3

He waited till he was halfway down a long slope before he spoke. "There's no love lost between you two, is there?" Fargo said.

"No," Toby admitted.

"You want to tell me about it?" he asked.

"When we get back to the house," she said. "Sam Tilton is finished by now. He lent me the mare." She led the way through a narrow passage bordered with a thick growth of the large yellow leaves and dark brown centers of Alpine sunflowers. The path turned out to be shortcut to the house. He followed her inside, where she stopped and stood silently in the center of the living room. He took in a cluttered room with large pieces of leather and hide scattered all over, a heavy table, and three thick-legged chairs at it. Seating in the rest of the room was plainly offered by collections of thick, brightly colored pillows that covered a good part of the floor. "It's hard, not seeing Amos here. Harder still knowing he won't ever be here again," she said.

"I'm sure it is," Fargo said.

She turned on him, and he saw the mist blue eyes were mistier than usual. "I'm going to hunt down that damn bear," she said.

"You keep away from that grizzly or you'll end up like Amos," Fargo said sternly. She turned and folded herself onto a nest of pillows, ponytail bouncing in unison with her breasts as she flounced herself down. She motioned to him, and he sat down beside her. "Now tell me about you and Elise Farrell," he said.

She leaned back on her hands, and her smallish breasts were firm as they pushed upward into her shirt. "Stu Farrell and Amos were good friends, real drinking buddies. They understood each other, and Stu admired Amos's work," Toby said.

"How does that figure on you and Elise?" Fargo asked.

"She was never a part of their relationship; I was," Toby Denison said.

"You saying she's jealous of you?"

"That's only part of it. The rest's more important. She thinks Stu may have given Amos the map," Toby said.

"Did he?" Fargo questioned.

"He might have," Toby said. "And she damn well knows that."

She fell silent, and Fargo saw a moment of smug satisfaction touch her pert, full-cheeked face.

"You're looking for it, too, aren't you?" he tossed at her.

It took her a moment to answer. "Yes," she said finally. "I've been looking for it. I haven't found it, though. Amos never knew I was looking for it."

"And you never told him," Fargo said. She nodded with a touch of embarrassment. "Why not? Why not just ask him? You said you were close."

"I tried, once, but Amos cut me off. He wouldn't hear any talk of it. And he wouldn't believe Elise would do anything to get hold of the map. You had to know Amos. He trusted people."

"But you knew better," Fargo said.

"I knew Elise. I knew she'd not stop at anything to get her hands on the map," Toby said.

"Elise thinks the map might be just a lot of scrawls and scribbles. Maybe there's really nothing at all," Fargo said.

"There's a map. I'm sure of it from the way Stu talked about it with Amos," Toby said firmly. "The longer Elise goes without finding it, the more she thinks it's here. I think it was one of her men that hit me when I came out of the barn. He was probably going after Amos, too, when the grizzly got there first."

"So they could search the place?" Fargo queried.

"That's right. It's be like her," Toby said.

"Or anybody," Fargo said. "I hear a lot of people knew about Stu Farrell's hidden mine and his secret map. He talked a lot, it seemed." She conceded the reality of what he'd said with silence and a half-grimace. "What else do you have against Elise Farrell?" Fargo asked.

"Isn't that enough?" Toby flared.

"It is, but there's more, something personal," Fargo said. "It's in your voice, your attitude. There's anger that comes from hating and anger that comes from hurting."

The mist blue eyes narrowed at him. "You're supposed to know about trails," she said.

"Some trails are made of grass and soil, some of wind and signs, and some of powder and paint," he said.

Her face took on a half-pout. "She always looked down at me, at Amos, too. She's always been a damn snob, thinking she's better than everybody else." Fargo smiled. He had his answer.

"You going to carry on here alone?" he asked.

"I don't know. I might. I'm not the craftsman Amos was."

"But you'll stay on."

"For now."

He gave her a slow smile. You're going to stay and look for the map, aren't you?" he queried.

"Why not?" she snapped. "I'd like to find it and the mine. I'm not rich. I'll turn this place upside down looking for it."

"Meanwhile, you don't want to end up like Amos. I'll stay the night, if you want. If that grizzly shows, maybe I can get him," Fargo said.

"I'd be real grateful to you for that," Toby said. "But I think you ought to warn the Carrigans, too. They're not far. Follow the valley south. They'll be the first place."

"You stay in till I get back. He probably won't show till dusk, but let's not take chances. Grizzlies are known to hunt anytime," Fargo said. She nodded and walked to the door with him, and suddenly he felt her lips against his cheek, a soft and fleeting touch.

"Thanks for helping. You're very nice. I'm only sorry you're going to work for that bitch," Toby said.

"I'll be back" he said, deciding not to mention Elise's ultimatum. She closed the door, and Fargo took the Ovaro into the shallow valley, turned south, and stayed in a trot until he reached a neat log house with sheep corrals stretching out behind it. He felt a sense of relief to see the two blond-haired children out front, and the woman came from the house as he rode to a halt, an older version of the children. The man appeared from behind the stable in moments, tall, well-built, and young, a ruggedly handsome face. "You the Carrigans?" Fargo asked, and the man nodded.

"Name's Fargo. I come with bad news," Fargo said and quickly told them about Amos's death and the grizzly.

"How awful," the woman said.

"Thought you ought to know, maybe move out till this killer's done in," Fargo said.

"That could be a long time," the man said.

"It could," Fargo admitted.

"I can't leave my stock alone that long. I'll stay," the man said.

"We'll stay with Ted," the woman said.

"I can take care of any bear," Ted Carrigan said.

"A rogue grizzly's not any bear. He's all power and all cunning. Even a buffalo rifle won't stop him unless you get off the perfect shot. Don't take this lightly."

"I don't, but I'm not running," the man said. "Thanks for the warning, though. I'll ride down to Amy Baker and warn her. She lives alone a mile down the valley. Same with Ed and Ann Wright. They're another half-mile west."

"That'd be good," Fargo said. "Luck to you." He turned the horse and started back to reach Toby's place as dusk began to settle. She came out wearing a blouse and a pair of denim overalls, looking both tomboyish and very feminine.

"You going to stable your horse?" she asked.

"I'll put him inside loose," Fargo said and led the Ovaro into the stable, unsaddled the horse, and let him roam free. Taking the big Henry with him, Fargo returned to the house and saw Toby had set a small table.

"Sit down. Got some dinner on," she said.

"That'd be good," Fargo said.

"I cleaned up the place some and got the extra room ready," Toby said.

"I'll bed down out here," Fargo said. "I'll be able to hear better." He cast a glance outside and saw the dusk was settling in fast, and he leaned the big Henry against the well. Toby served a stew of buffalo meat with onions and carrots that proved to be tasty and hearty. She talked of various things with delightful youth and vivacity, and suddenly death and hidden maps seemed very far away. But they weren't, and he had just finished the meal when he was reminded of that fact as his head snapped up. "He's back. Turn the lamp off," Fargo said.

"I didn't hear anything," Toby said, shutting the lamp down.

"Neither did I, but I smell him," Fargo said, his nostrils twitching. "There's only one odor like bear." He opened the window from the bottom and rested the rifle barrel on the sill. It was but moments later that he heard the beat of the Ovaro's hooves as the horse fled out of the barn to the safety of space and darkness. Toby came up and knelt beside Fargo, and he saw she held a big Remington Beals six-shot single action. It could deliver a powerful shot, but it wouldn't be much against a big grizzly. The moon had come up to bathe the area in a pale light, and the odor of the bear was strong now. He wasn't far away, and Fargo heard his huge form moving through the hackberry near the barn. The creature moved alongside the barn, shifted direction, and then Fargo heard the noise from behind the house.

He felt Toby tense against him, and he rested one hand on her leg. "Relax," he said.

"You think he knows we're in here?" she whispered.

"He knows. He smells us, just as we smell him," Fargo said.

"But he's not trying to break in," Toby breathed.

"He senses danger. He has his own ways. Grizzlies are very careful," Fargo said, then fell silent, his ears straining to catch every little sound. He heard only faint shuffling steps and then tree branches being brushed back, but slowly and steadily. "He's leaving," Fargo said, pushing the window open wide. He swung long legs over the windowsill and raised the rifle to his shoulder. The stand of hackberry rose alongside the end of the barn, but Fargo glimpsed the dark form inside the thick trees.

He raised the rifle and fired as the giant form vanished, reappeared, and vanished again inside the forest. He fired the big Henry, one shot after another, until the rifle was emptied and the sound of the shots faded away, and he could barely hear the grizzly moving away through the forest. He swung back into the room and closed the window. "I thought you said only a perfect shot exactly in the right place would stop him," Toby said. "You fired off a barrage."

"I was trying to scare him off, raise enough ruckus to make him go someplace else," Fargo said.

"You don't sound confident," Toby said, and he uttered a wry grunt. She was too perceptive.

"One for you," he muttered. "He'll stay away tonight, maybe longer, but I wouldn't take bets on that. He killed here. That'll stay with him."

She turned up the lamp and showed him to a small room with a cot in it and a lone window. "Nothing fancy, I'm afraid," she said.

"Indoors is fancy," Fargo said.

"You want help finding your horse?" she asked.

"No, he'll make his way back when he feels it's safe. He's one very smart horse," Fargo said.

"Thanks again for everything, and for staying," Toby said, and again her lips brushed his cheek, but he caught her arm before she turned away.

"You're getting to make a habit of that," he said.

"I'll try to stop," she said. "Or do better." She offered a sly little smile as she left, her compact rear swaying with youthful firmness. He undressed, stretched out on the cot, and quickly slept until morning came to flood the little room with light. He went outside to a small well and washed. Toby appeared when he finished, wearing an oversize shirt over Levi's that made her look even more like a little girl. Only the very sultry mist blue eyes gave the lie to that as they traveled across the smooth contours of his muscled torso with obvious appreciation.

"Amos painted and drew people whenever he got the chance. He'd have loved to draw you," Toby said.

"You paint, too?" he asked.

"A little, not like Amos, though."

"Never posed for an artist before," Fargo said.

"We could make it a first," Toby said.

"Maybe, but we'll make that grizzly the first order of business. You ought to leave here till he's gone or done in. There must be someplace you can go," Fargo said.

"Not really. There's Amy Baker, but staying with her would be no safer than staying here."

"We'll rig up an alarm for you," he said. "Get all the tin pails you have while I finish dressing." She nodded and hurried off to return with six pails and four wooden buckets. "We put small stones in each, just enough to fill the bottom. Then we string the pails together with wire or rope and put them in a circle around the house."

"Anyone or anything approaching the house will trip the wire and set the rocks rattling in the pails," Toby finished.

"It'll give you a warning, time to get inside, bolt the doors or hide. Help me rig it, and then I'll see if I can pick up his tracks," Fargo said. She hurried along with him, and after they had the crude alarm system in place, she served biscuits and coffee. "I'll look in on you later," he said, and she held his arm as he walked outside, whistled, and watched the Ovaro trot into sight from behind the barn. He saddled the horse, and she waved as he rode away, putting the Ovaro into a low jump to clear the wire of the alarm. He steered the horse into the hackberry and quickly picked up the huge paw prints until they came to an end at a wide, strong-running stream. He saw where the grizzly had caught and eaten a half-dozen rainbow trout and left the heads on the stream bank.

He'd gone on through the stream, ending the trail. Fargo turned away and rode across a low rise when he saw a rider coming toward him, short black hair bouncing. Elise Farrell pulled to a halt on a gray gelding, dismounted, and Fargo swung from the Ovaro. Her willowy figure, dramatically attractive in a black shirt and black denim trousers, her eyes fixed on him as she halted only inches from him. "Been looking for you. Figured you might be up here searching for tracks," she said.

"You figured right," he said.

"I'm sorry," she said. "I was all wrong. I'd no right to talk to you that way. I've been on edge, not finding anything. I've been tight as a rubber band stretched too far."

"Confession's good for the soul, they say," Fargo remarked.

"I want your help. I need you. Forget everything I said. You do whatever you want. Just help me find that mine," she said.

His eyes searched her face. "I believe you mean it," he said. He felt surprise and couldn't help admiring her directness. It was a kind of honesty not often found.

"I do mean it. Stay, help me. Please," she said. "And there's the rest of your fee when we find the mine."

"I did come a long way. No sense in letting all that time go to waste," he said, and suddenly her mouth was on his, the slightly thin lips pressing hard, her breasts touching his chest. Perhaps they weren't so shallow, he reflected.

"Proof I mean it, if words aren't enough," Elise said.

"A little extra proof never hurts," he said. She stepped back, a smile edging her lips as she pulled herself onto the gelding. "But I do intend checking in on Toby Denison so long as I can," Fargo added. "She's sitting on a powder keg called rogue grizzly."

"I told you, do whatever you want. Just help me," she said. "And don't expect too much of me."

"Meaning what exactly?"

"I don't want to see anyone torn apart by a grizzly, but don't expect me to be concerned over her," Elise said, her voice taking on its usual imperiousness.

Fargo studied her for another moment. "You're afraid Stu left the map with Amos," he said, and she shrugged. "The grizzly didn't hit her on the head."

"She say I'm responsible for that?" Elise snapped.

"She thinks it could be."

"I told you, half the roughnecks in town know about the map. Stu talked too damn much. I'd nothing to do with her getting hit," Elise said.

He continued to study her. "It's more than the map, isn't it?" he asked and saw Elise's face tighten as he climbed onto the Ovaro and rode beside her. "Let's have all of it," he pressed.

"She was entirely too cozy with Stu," the woman said. "Of course, she didn't know he was past being seduced, way past. But she was trying. She's really quite a greedy, clutching little thing. Don't let that wide-eyed youthful innocence fool you."

"I won't," Fargo said and smiled inwardly. He'd gotten one thing clear. The dislike wasn't all Toby's. They both wanted the map and to find the mine. Greed made them adversaries, but jealousy and pure bitchiness made them enemies. "You all out of places to look?" he asked Elise as they rode to her spread.

"Almost, but there's one place. Stu stored some furniture in a shed behind the stable. I haven't moved it to look there yet," she said.

"Why not?" Fargo queried.

"It's the last place I can think of. I didn't want to be alone with Rick Chowder or the others when I look there," she said.

"That sounds as though you don't trust them too much," Fargo said.

"I do, up to a point. I hired them only a few months back. I don't really know any of them," she said.

"You don't really know me," he put in.

"You come with a reputation, and I trust you, something about you, a feeling I get," she said. "Now that you're here I'll look there. You can help move things for me."

The ranch house came into sight, and Fargo saw the four men outside, positioned in different places that let them cover all the approaches. He exchanged nods with Rick Chowder as he dismounted and followed Elise behind the stable. A rear room held a jumble of pieces of furniture, old lamps, tables, heavy chairs, and assorted pieces of lumber that included broken half-tables and two-legged chairs. It wouldn't be quickly moved, he saw, and he shed his jacket and shirt and saw Elise's eyes on him. "Join me? It'll be a hot job," he said dryly and she allowed a half-smile.

"Maybe another time," she said and began to move a piece of two-by-four. Fargo attacked the collection of furniture, moving each piece out of the room and to the rear of the stable. When he finally finished, Elise working beside him, her shirt was wet and clung to her breasts. They were indeed shallow, but nonetheless held a lovely concave curve to them that ended in full cups that pressed against the material. With the outer pieces removed, the room held two old wooden desks, a battered dresser, a smaller but equally batter bureau, four big barrels, and two lamps with glass shades.

"Where'd he collect all this old stuff?" Fargo queried.

"Stu loved old furniture and antiques. What money he didn't gamble away he spent on buying old junk," Elise said. "I'll be days taking apart all this."

"It'll be dark soon. Maybe you'd best wait till morning to start," Fargo said.

"Good idea. Come into the house, and you can freshen up," she said. Shirt and jacket in one hand, he followed her from the back of the stable and into the house. She led him to a large room at the rear of the house where a deep basin of clear water, a washcloth, and towels lay alongside the bedroom dresser. Beyond it, a large double bed with a pink comforter and a tall dressing screen of matching pink gave the room a very feminine feel. He used the washcloth along with a bar of soft soap, aware that Elise watched from near the dressing screen. When he toweled himself dry, she stepped behind the screen for a moment. When she reappeared, the black shirt was unbuttoned, and he saw the long edge of one curving breast. "You're finished. Good. I'm feeling terribly sticky," she said.

He half smiled as his gaze stayed on the convex curve, perhaps more provocative for being only a glimpse. "You saying something more?" he asked.

"I'm saying you might be worth showing more," she said.

"I'll remember that," he said. "I'll see you in the morning."

"Make sure all you do is check in on her," Elise said.

"Trust me," Fargo said.

"That's asking a lot," Elise said and stepped behind the screen as he left. Outside, he rode from the house as the day began to recede and made a detour to arrive at Toby's, carefully guided the pinto over the alarm wires, and let his eyes and nose survey the territory. He was grateful to find no signs of bear, and Toby came from the house, hands on her hips, and regarded him with a wry smile.

"Staying or passing?" she asked.

"Passing," he said.

"Orders from your boss?" she asked tartly.

"No, I'm going to pay a visit to town. If trouble's coming from there, maybe I can sniff it out," he said. "Maybe I can stop back again later."

"I'd like that," she said. "Staying in, being so careful, it makes me feel trapped."

"Let's hope we can put an end to that soon," he said.

"Elise hasn't found the map yet," Toby said with a touch of smugness.

"What makes you so sure of that?" he asked.

"You wouldn't be here. You'd be off searching for the mine," she said.

"You haven't, either, I'd say," Fargo returned, and she crinkled her nose. He waved and moved on as dusk began to fall. Making a wide circle, he searched the area as dusk turned to darkness, but saw no sign of bear, so he turned the pinto northward. He arrived at Hobsonville, reined up in front of the saloon, and tethered the horse to the far end of a hitching rail. He strolled into the saloon and took in a half-dozen round tables, a sawdust-covered floor, and a bar against one wall, a row of liquor bottles behind the bartender. It was a very ordinary small-town saloon, and he heard the murmur of voices dwindle almost to silence as he stepped up to the bar where three figures made room for him.

"Bourbon," he said to the barkeep, a short, chubby-faced man with a sizable paunch hanging over the top of his bartender's apron. "Guess you don't get many strangers in here," Fargo remarked as the almost total silence deepened.

"Some," the bartender said.

"That ain't the reason, mister," a voice interjected, and Fargo took a sip of not very good bourbon before he turned. A man stepped forward, clothed in a shirt without sleeves, a fat yet big figure with heavy, treelike arms, a huge chest and protruding stomach, and a head that seemed to sit on his shoulders without a neck in between. "You ain't just a stranger. You're the one come to find that map for Elise Farrell," the man said through thick

50

lips, his face heavy and jowly with beetle black eyebrows.

"How do you know that?" Fargo asked calmly.

"We've got our ways," the man said.

"Who're you, mister?" Fargo inquired.

"They call me Big Jake," the man said.

"Well, Big Jake, how's this any of your business?" Fargo questioned and saw most of the men in the saloon step back against the walls. But five stayed in a half-circle behind Big Jake.

"It's our business because we've got our own plans for getting that mine," the man growled. Fargo's eyes moved across the room again. Most of the others were no threat. Big Jake and his five cronies formed the threat, he decided. He kept his manner unruffled as he gave a half-shrug.

"Seeing as how it's Elise Farrell's, I don't think you boys have any claim," Fargo said.

"It's not hers. Stu Farrell used to come in here and drink with us. He said the mine belonged to anybody who could find it," Big Jake said.

"And you think you can find it," Fargo said.

"We aim to try," the man said.

"But you don't mean find it. You mean steal it," Fargo said.

The man's heavy face darkened. "Don't get smart with me. You can forget about helping Elise Farrell, and ride away from here in one piece," he said.

"Or else?"

"A man can get himself killed picking a fight in a saloon," Big Jake said.

"Is that what I've done?" Fargo smiled.

"Looks that way to me, right, boys?" Big Jake said, and the five behind him murmured agreement. Fargo's eyes had become the blue of an ice floe as he surveyed the men in front of him. The hulk's arms were too heavy for him to make even a reasonably fast draw, and the other five were too ordinary to be much better, their holsters cracked and worn. His hand moved to the Colt at his hip.

"You boys should know I'll have a bullet in each of you before anyone gets a gun out," Fargo said calmly. "Don't make me prove it."

"Get your hand off that gun," a voice cut in, and Fargo flicked a glance at the bartender. The man held an army carbine aimed at him from over the bar. "Drop your gun belt," the bartender said. Fargo eyed the carbine again. There was no way the man could miss. He cursed silently as he unhooked the buckle and the gun belt fell to the ground. "Kick it over here," the bartender said, and Fargo obeyed. "I don't allow gunplay in my place," the man said. "A fair fight breaks out, that's something else."

"Fair fight?" Fargo snorted.

The bartender didn't answer, but Big Jake started forward, his treelike arms rising. They intended to beat him to death, or to a crippled pulp, and it'd be an accident, one more saloon brawl with the witnesses all backing up each other. Fargo tensed his every muscle and rose on the balls of his feet as Big Jake suddenly charged, swinging a roundhouse right. Fargo easily ducked the blow and countered with a short right that exploded on the man's jaw. The blow would've decked most men, and it did snap Big Jake's head back and stopped him in his tracks. Fargo's left hook followed instantly, and this time Big Jake's head turned sideways and he dropped to one knee.

"Sonofabitch," another voice said, and Fargo saw two of the others as Big Jake stayed on one knee, shaking his head. Fargo ducked away from the one on his left, spun, avoided a wild swing from the second one, and brought around a right hook that sent the man to the floor. But the other one barreled into him in a waist-high tackle. Fargo let himself go backward with the man's attack and brought his knee up. "Ow, Jesus," the man cried out as he went down clutching his groin. But Big Jake was up, swinging the treelike arms as he came forward, and Fargo felt the power of the huge arms as he parried the blows. He ducked low and brought a tremendous blow into Big Jake's paunch. The man's breath left him in an explosive gasp, and he half fell forward. Fargo glimpsed one of the other two picking himself up from the floor and aimed a sideways kick. The man dropped to the floor again, and Fargo whirled to see the other three had been triggered into action.

They rushed him in unison, and Fargo spun on his left, brought down a chopping blow, and one of the three fell facedown. Spinning, head down, Fargo lashed out with a left and a right, and another figure went down. But two leaped onto his back, and he fell forward, tried to roll away, and felt the kicks catch him in the ribs. He cursed in pain, rolled, and came against heavy legs. He had time only to see Big Jake bring both hands down, all his bulk behind the double-fisted blow. Fargo twisted his body and managed to avoid the full force of the blow, but took enough to feel wracking pain shoot through his body. Another foot kicked and caught him in the temple, and he felt the rush of red warmth course down his face. He tried to get up, but arms clutched at his legs, and then he was sailing through the air, tossed as if he were a child.

He came down on one of the round tables, felt it smash and splinter under him, and hit the floor on his back, half across the table. Fargo saw Big Jake looming over him and starting to reach down to seize him again, one of the others beside him. The heavy face was suddenly wavy as the pain swirled through him, but Fargo felt the table leg under his hand, curled fingers around it, and thrust it upward, driving the splintered end of it into the heavy face. "Owooo . . . ow, goddamn," Big Jake swore as, both hands clutched to his face, he staggered backward, streaming blood and curses. But the others leaped on Fargo as he tried to roll away. He was pulled back and felt the deluge of fists and feet that rained down on him.

One of them used the edge of the table to smash it into his ribs, and Fargo felt his flesh tear and the blood instantly soak his shirt. He knew the wave of weakness as it swept over him, and he realized they were going to kill him in their fury. With the desperation only the will to survive can summon, he managed to reach down to his leg and pull the double-edged throwing knife from its calf holster. As more blows rained down on him, he swung the knife upward, then sideways, then in a flat arc and then thrusting with it again. The figures fell away with garbled cries, and Fargo felt the blood spray over him, soaking his shirt, mingling in with his own blood.

He pushed to his feet and saw the jumble of figures scattered around the floor, some with stillness of death, some clutching at their sides. Big Jake, a kerchief held to his face, started toward him. Fighting away the dizziness,

Fargo stepped sideways, feinted, and came up behind the big man, pressing the blade to his throat. He peered past Big Jake to where the bartender still held the carbine. "Drop it or I cut his ugly head off and do the world a favor," he growled.

The barkeep hesitated a second, then let the carbine drop on the other side of the bar. "Easy, now," he muttered, but Fargo kept the blade pressed to Big Jake's throat.

"Walk," he said, and the man staggered forward, holding the kerchief to his face. "Outside," Fargo said as he fought off a wave of weakness.

"Don't kill me," Big Jake pleaded.

"Don't make the wrong move," Fargo said, pressing against the hulk as they moved from the saloon. When they reached the Ovaro, Fargo pulled the knife away and smashed a fist into Big Jake's back. The man went down on both knees, then collapsed onto his face. Fargo pulled himself onto the horse, clutched the saddle horn, and fought off a wave of dizziness, then sent the horse forward. The pain consumed him as he kept the horse at a walk, steered south along a narrow road.

The moon stayed ahead of him, a pale guide as he kept the pinto along the edge of the forest. He leaned forward, his face contorted in pain, his entire body on fire. Toby's place was the nearest, but he cursed as he realized he mightn't be able to last long enough to get there. Strangely enough, his bloodied, battered, bruised body did best when he managed to sit straight in the saddle. But the waves of weakness continued to sweep over him, each one bringing him closer to passing out. The moon began to dip down beyond the mountains as he kept the pinto moving, fighting to recognize marks, find ridges, retrace steps. Pain turned time into meaningless agony, but finally he was sure he was drawing closer to Toby's place. But the last of his strength gave out as he moved through the forest of hackberry. He felt himself slide from the saddle, the trees spinning away as he fell heavily to the forest floor. He lay facedown, and the trees stopping spinning as the world faded away.

4

Morning and Fargo's first groan of consciousness came together. He slowly opened his eyes, lifted his head, and felt the pain shoot through his body. He blinked and let his eyes swim into focus, then saw the softness of the morning stretch out in front of him, the little droplets of lungwort, stretches of rosinweed with their yellow caps, and tall stands of sweet clover mixed in with hackberry and box elder. Pushing up on the flat of his hands, he grimaced in pain as he sat up and felt the half-caked blood that soaked his shirt and body. He had just fought off a wave of pain when he heard the sound. Even through his blood-soaked nose the odor came to him, distinctive, unmistakable, musky yet much more powerful, a cloying, dense heaviness to it.

"Aw, Jesus," Fargo murmured as he ignored the pain to push to his feet and peer into the forest. The huge form quickly took shape, lumbering through the foliage. Big, heavy snout lifted upward, the grizzly was sniffing the air as he moved forward with his slightly swaying motion. He had caught the odor of blood, Fargo realized, and his keen nose now zeroed in on the scent. Fargo cast a quick glance to find the Ovaro, but the horse had already moved out of sight at the first appearance of the grizzly. Another quick glance showed Fargo that the giant bear was moving toward him, massive head upraised, gathering speed as he bore in on the scent. Cursing with pain, Fargo pulled his shirt off. He had to buy time, offer the monstrous bear distractions, find a way to flee to safety. Holding the blood-soaked shirt, he flung it with what strength he had and saw it land a half-dozen yards left of the grizzly.

The bear halted, sniffed, and turned at once, instantly following his new, closer scent, and Fargo had already begun to run. He kept running, a pain-filled hobble, and glanced back to see the grizzly had reached the blood-soaked shirt. The bear scooped up the shirt, sniffed at it, bit into it, and took it into his mouth while he put one huge paw on the other end of the garment and pulled. The shirt came apart, and the grizzly tore it into shreds as he shook his massive head. Fargo fell to one knee, his breath a hoarse, gasping sound, then let himself gather wind again and continued on. Another glance back showed him he had bought another three or four minutes at most, and he ran blindly, brushing against low branches, crashing through tall underbrush.

The grizzly followed again, his nose and his ears providing him with everything he needed to close in on his quarry. Pausing again, Fargo leaned against the trunk of a hackberry and pulled off his blood-stained trousers. He threw the garment back into the trees and ran on. He had bought himself another few minutes, he knew, but only that. The grizzly would follow the distraction, sniff it, mouth it, and then tear it apart as he had the shirt, and go on, more determined than before. The bear would cover ground very quickly, his cumbersome appearance a fatal deception, and Fargo cursed as he had to pause again, his bruised body demanding relief. But he pushed himself on and realized the land had grown steep. He was climbing uphill, and another glance behind showed the grizzly coming after him, plowing through the thick foliage as if it didn't exist. Fargo used the low branches to keep himself going, painfully aware that the bear was drawing closer.

He reached the top of the slope and saw the trees thinning out at his right, then swerved and found new strength to push faster. The direction brought him to the end of the hackberry stand where a deep, narrow ravine dropped hundreds of feet to a rocky bottom. He moved along the edge of the deep ravine, the trees at his back, and now he could hear the grizzly's breathy growls. Fargo peered down at the steep side of the ravine, went on another hundred yards as the sound of the bear grew louder, and halted when he saw the ledge some ten feet below the top edge of the ravine, a narrow stone outcropping not more than a foot wide.

His eyes went to the steep side of the ravine just over the ledge, and he saw the wiry strands of mountain brush that grew from the tiny fissures and cracks in the rock. The grizzly had come out of the trees, some fifty yards behind, but in full view, and for the first time Fargo got an unobstructed view of the animal's massive power. But the grizzly saw him also and, lowering its head, began to come at a swaying but ground-eating lope. Fargo glanced down at the narrow ledge below the top edge of the ravine and knew it was his only chance. Grasping one of the wiry lengths of mountain brush, he let himself drop down over the edge of the ravine. The brush bent at once from his weight, but it held, and he took hold of another stemlike strand that protruded out of the rock and let himself down further, pressing himself against the side of the ravine.

Another, thicker growth of shrub grew outward, and he grabbed hold of it and lowered himself again until he felt his feet touch the narrow ledge, just barely wide enough for him to stand on with his body pressed against the steep side of the rock face. He halted, clinging to the brush with both hands, and slowly let his head go backward enough to be able to peer up the side of the ravine. The huge muzzle and head stared down at him, the grizzly stopped at the very edge of the ravine directly over the ledge. The grizzly snarled and drew its lips back. Fargo saw two-inch fangs and claws at least five inches long. The grizzly growled, a low, terrifying sound and swayed back and forth as he peered down at his prey. He snarled, showing the huge yellow-white fangs, and beat a soft, shuffling tattoo with his forepaws in frustration.

The bear sensed there was no way he could climb down to his quarry without falling headfirst into the ravine. Natural wisdom told him that and added to his fury. He growled, fumed, shuffled, and snarled. Finally, he halted his frustrated movements and lowered his forequarters to the ground. Reaching down with his right foreleg, he swept one huge paw from left to right, back and forth, straining as far as he dared without losing balance. Fargo saw the tremendous claws passing over his head, fully extended, and knew that only an inch separated his head from the ripping, tearing paw that would send him plunging down the ravine. With the stubborn tenacity of his species, the grizzly kept swinging the huge paw as he tried to rip claws through Fargo's scalp. But he couldn't reach that last inch, and his growls grew louder and angrier.

Fargo felt his own strength slipping away. His fingers were locked, the only reason he still clung to the ledge. But they would come apart soon, he knew, snap open to send him plunging to the bottom of the ravine. But if he pulled himself upward and tried to flex his fingers, the tremendous claws would tear through his scalp. He cursed in pain and helplessness. His lips were pulled back as he wondered how long he could hold on. His hands trembled, and he knew his fingers would soon unlock, and he cursed again when suddenly he saw the paw had stopped swinging back and forth over his head. He shifted his eyes upward and saw that the bear had retreated from the edge.

As Fargo watched, the grizzly slowly turned and walked away. The massive head rose into the air and emitted a deep, growling roar, and Fargo recognized it for what it was, a promise. The grizzly disappeared from view, and Fargo licked lips that had become dry as old parchment. Yet he somehow held on until the sound of the bear faded away. Using every last ounce of strength, he managed to uncramp his fingers and pull himself up on the stalk of wiry brush. Pausing to rest, fighting off the pain of his bruised body and of muscles now stretched to the breaking point, he pulled again, found another piece of brush, and clung to it until he finally reached the top of the ravine. He lay there, gasping in air until a measure of strength began to flow through him again.

He pushed to his feet and began to retrace steps into the trees. Waves of dizziness continued to sweep over him, each one harder to fight off. He hadn't gone far when he saw the familiar form coming toward him through the trees, and he halted till the Ovaro reached him. Holding onto the saddle horn, Fargo pulled himself onto the horse and moved south through the forest, only dimly aware that he wore only boots and undershorts. Pain forced him to close his eyes every few minutes, yet he kept on, clinging to the horse, his clouded eyes peering through the trees, seeking out markers to find his way. He was not aware that the hackberry had begun to thin out and the land opened to a clear area. Even his iron constitution had its limits. He felt himself falling forward.

He tried to cling to the powerful jet black neck, but his hands slid away and he toppled from the horse. For a dim, fleeting moment he thought he heard a clattering sound as he hit the ground and passed out.

5

Warmth. Soothing softness. Pleasure instead of pain. The feelings sifted through his mind as consciousness returned. Slowly, he forced his eyes open, and the sensations translated themselves from amorphous feelings into form and definition. He became aware of hands moving across his back, his shoulders, waist, buttocks, legs. He stirred, and a groan escaped him. "Welcome back," a voice said, and he turned his head to see Toby standing over him. He lay on the cot, he saw, her hands gently massaging his body, and he felt the cool touch of the salve on his skin and detected the faint aroma of wintergreen.

"Feels good, real good," Fargo murmured.

"Balm of Gilead, comfrey, and wintergreen compress," Toby said. "The best ointment in the world of bruises and muscle pain." He sighed as her hands moved across his body, soft yet firm, a warm, sensual touch. "You're good at this. Practice?" he asked.

"Used to rub Amos's old muscles," she said.

"How'd I get here?" he asked.

"Your horse tripped the alarm wire. I grabbed my gun and looked out and saw you," she said. "You were hard to drag all the way here."

"I'll bet," Fargo said. "Where's my horse?"

"Loose in the stable, along with mine. I remember what you said. I'm quick to learn." Toby's hands moved down over his tight buttocks, lingered as they massage, then down to the back of his legs. "What happened?" she asked. "You've taken a lot of punishment."

"First some unpleasant gents in town," he said and told her of the attack in the saloon. "Then the goddamn grizzly found me."

"My God, it's a wonder you're here and alive," Toby said as she massaged more salve onto his back. "How'd you manage to get away from the grizzly?"

"Found a ledge where he couldn't reach me," Fargo said, then fell silent with his own thoughts. With her quickness she saw he was suddenly not with her.

"What are you thinking about?" she asked.

"Something I don't want to believe," he said.

"That's not saying a lot."

"It'll do for now," he said.

Toby drew hands from him. "Sleep as long as you can," she said. She had no need to urge him as sleep descended on him the moment he closed his eyes. He slept the deep slumber of the battered and exhausted to finally wake knowing not how many hours had gone by, but only that the burning pain was gone from his body. He turned, still found himself wincing, and saw he was still buck naked. But he saw his undershorts hanging over the back of a nearby chair, and he stood up, managed to draw on his undershorts when he felt himself collapsing back onto the cot. His body definitely cried out for more rest, and he turned his head as Toby came into the room. "Heard you," she said, her eyes moving over him. "It's a little late for modesty," she said.

"Wasn't modesty. I was going to get up," he said. "Guess I'm not ready for that. But I do hurt a lot less, thanks to you and that salve. I owe you."

She shrugged. "I enjoyed it," she said. "Maybe more than I should have."

"Oh?" he said, and she returned a Cheshire cat smile. "Or maybe not enough," he said. She allowed another shrug. "Give me till morning," he said.

The Cheshire cat smile widened. "Then you'd best get back to sleep," she said and hurried from the room. He closed his eyes, and sleep again came at once, plunging him into its depths. He stayed hard asleep as the night came again, and it was the clatter of stones in the pails that snapped his eyes open. He started to push himself up when he heard the voices, Toby's first, then the clipped, brusqueness of Elise.

"Let me see him," Elise demanded, and Fargo heard the footsteps coming toward him. He closed his eyes, let his body relax, and lay still. Elise's voice came again. "What the hell is this?" she snapped.

"Don't wake him. Keep your voice down," Toby returned.

"Enjoy yourselves?" Fargo heard Elise hiss.

"Look again. He's almost unconscious. He was badly beaten," Toby said. Elise was silent, but Fargo felt her eyes going over him. "He'll need more rest," Toby said.

"He can get it at my place. I hired him. I'll see to him," Elise said. "I'll be back with a wagon in the morning." Fargo remained motionless as he heard her hurry out. Only after she left did he open his eyes and wait until Toby returned. She came in wearing a short, light nightdress, high, round breasts pushing the top out and poking two tiny points in the thin fabric. She halted beside him.

"Go back to sleep. You need the rest," she said, one hand warm against his chest.

"Concern or anticipation?" he murmured, and her little smile was enigmatic. He returned to sleep, and this time woke only when dawn seeped into the little room. He stretched and was quietly amazed at how much better he felt when Toby entered, still in the light nightdress. She carried a basin of water and a cloth. "You're up early." he said.

"I want to clean the salve off you," she said, and he watched her as she began to wash his body with the cloth, the water soothing, her touch gentle, and when she leaned forward, he could see the tops of the small but very round breasts.

"Nursing or enjoying?" he asked.

"Both," she said, finishing, then using another cloth to dry him. He let her do whatever she wanted, and when she finished, she set down the little vial of ointment and returned to the cot, put both hands against his chest, leaned forward, and her lips were suddenly on his, soft and sweet. Then he felt her move and sink onto the cot beside him. She drew her lips back, lifted both arms, and the nightdress came off over her head, and the very round, small breasts suddenly seemed larger than they were. Their firm roundness pushed forward with their own boldness, each tipped by a pale pink, small nipple on an even paler pink circle. A round, barrel chest lay just below their perky loveliness followed by a short, slightly chunky waist, a round belly and a wavy, densely black triangle. Sturdy, pink-fleshed thighs vibrated with youthful firmness, and smoothly round knees contoured into strong calves.

Toby brought herself half over him, round high breasts pressing firmly into his chest. He brought his arms up to encircle her, but she stopped him. "Let me," she murmured. "You relax. I'll do the rest." She moved, rubbing her body against his as she brought her breasts up over his face, wiggled to bring one little mound onto his mouth, and pressed its softness down, pushing his lips open. "Take it . . . take it, yes, oh, God, yes," Toby murmured, and she pressed her breast deeper into his mouth. He felt the pale pink tip grow firmer as he caressed it with his tongue, and she moaned, then finally pulled the breast away and gave him the other. Finally, she drew back and slid her body downward against his, bringing warm little kisses in a path across his muscled chest, pausing at each nipple, then going on using lips, tongue, hands, everything arousing and tingling.

She continued, her lips tracing their own path down his body, over his abdomen, down again, slowing at his groin. He felt her fingers reach down and curl around him, then he felt something else, his own pulsating hotness aroused, seeking, waiting. He heard his own gasp of pleasure as she smothered, nuzzled, kissed, caressed, stroked, and encompassed him in a torrent of sweet sensations. She made little gurgling noises of delight, and suddenly she brought her firm rear around, the round belly coming down atop him, the densely black triangle pushing hard into his groin. She came over him, straddling, full, young, pink-fleshed thighs pressed hard against his hips, and then she was moving, up and down, thrusting all of herself, up and down, tiny half-cries of utter pleasure coming from her.

Toby's head lifted, her eyes closed and her mouth open, the small, round breasts bouncing firmly in unison as she bucked and plunged, each movement more violent than the one before, each gasp more filled with ecstasy. She suddenly fell forward, breasts coming down onto his face as her torso bucked with new abandon. "Yes, yes, yes, yes," she half screamed and seemed to be gritting her teeth, and then he felt her thighs grow tight against him, her cries almost strangled. Suddenly, she was quivering against him, fingers digging into him, and he felt his own body erupting, sensations spiraling beyond his control. "Oh, God, now, now, aaaaiiiii, yes, now," Toby screamed, and Fargo felt that moment captured, imprinted indelibly yet evanescently, shared sensations, bondings of eros too intense to endure more than moments.

With an almost angry cry Toby went limp, her thighs straightening, legs pushing backward and her body falling over his. She stayed atop him, tiny quivers finally fading away, and her arms encircled his neck, breasts against his face. "You all right?" he asked, and she nodded. "Shows you what a little first aid can lead to," he remarked, and she pushed her head up and stared down at him, the Cheshire cat smile on her lips again.

"I didn't want you to strain muscles or use up energy. I wanted to do everything," she said.

"You did real well," he said. "Next time it's my turn."

"What makes you think there'll be a next time?" she asked.

"What makes you think there won't be?" he countered.

"Maps, mines, Elise," she said, swinging her firm, young body from the cot with more exuberance than grace.

"I'm good at finding ways," Fargo said as he rose. "I'd best get dressed. I've a clean outfit in my pack." Toby slipped on her nightdress as he walked outside where the Ovaro came at his whistle. He took a shirt and Levi's from his pack, dressed, and returned to the house. Toby waited, now in a white shirt and blue denims, and had two mugs of coffee on the table. He had just finished his when the stones set up a loud clatter, and he was at the window instantly to see Elise driving up in a buckboard with yellow wheels.

"Your carriage," Toby muttered, sarcasm heavy in her tone.

"Thanks for everything." Fargo said, and gave her a quick hug. "Don't get careless about that grizzly," he said sternly. She nodded gravely and stayed inside as he walked from the house. Elise stared at him, her brows lifting.

"You make a quick recovery," she said.

"Looks are deceiving. I still hurt," he said and tied the Ovaro behind the buckboard before stepping beside her into the rig.

"You can finish recuperating at my place. You'll have less distraction," Elise said curtly, snapping the reins over the horse.

He shot her with a long, sideways glance. "Maybe you're being too modest," he said.

"It's not modesty. It's principles. I don't take advantage of someone for my own pleasure," Elise said.

"You think she'd do that?" Fargo asked mildly.

"I sure do. You're lucky you were out most of the time," Elise said.

"Guess so," Fargo agreed and sat back as Elise drove alone a narrow road that finally ended up at her place.

"You haven't said anything about finding the map," he said. "You go through everything?"

"Got a few pieces left," Elise said. "I can finish them by tomorrow."

"I found out something. This place is being watched. They knew I'd arrived," Fargo told her and saw surprise and alarm on her face.

"My God. What do we do about that?" Elise asked.

"Nothing," Fargo said.

"I don't like it. I feel spied on," she said.

"It'd be hard to stop. You'd need a platoon patrolling," Fargo said.

"I still don't like it," she said as he followed her into a spacious bedroom, the walls hung with drapes, the dresser freshly varnished, a bed covered with fresh sheets. "You can rest all you like here. I'll be back to look in on you," Elise said.

"Obliged," Fargo said, and Elise hurried away. He shed his shorts and boots and stretched out on the bed. He felt immensely better, but his body told him it would welcome another few hours of rest. Closing his eyes, he let himself sleep, and when he woke, the sun had crossed into the afternoon. He dressed and left the room to find Elise in the living room. She turned in surprise to see him, a cup of coffee in her hand.

"Thought you'd sleep the day through," she said and offered him a cup of coffee.

"I'm well enough to collect my gun," he said as he sipped the coffee.

"You're not going back into town, are you?" Elise frowned.

"It won't be the same," Fargo said, and she came over to stand very close.

"Be careful, please. I'm getting more afraid and more discouraged. I need support, and that means you," she said. She sounded honestly troubled, all the authoritativeness suddenly deserting her.

"I'll be fine, trust me," he said. Her eyes searched his face, concern in their brown depths, and she slid arms around his neck and clung to him for a long moment before stepping back and hurrying away. He walked outside and swung onto the Ovaro to ride away, thinking about Elise Farrell and Toby. Both could surprise, and both could turn unexpected faces—Toby exchanging sweet, open youthfulness for sudden boldness, Elise replacing imperiousness for sudden vulnerability. Or were they simply being female, he wondered as he moved the Ovaro toward the town. His musings were cut off as a single horseman appeared from the line of serviceberry, riding hard.

Fargo recognized Ted Carrigan as the man drew closer and skidded his horse to halt, his face flushed and shaken. "Goddamn grizzly killed Amy Baker," the man shouted. "Found her in pieces, torn apart. It was horrible."

"When?" Fargo asked.

"Couple of hours ago, I'd guess," Ted Carrigan said.

"Where's your family?" Fargo questioned.

"Locked inside the house. I'm going to get Sam Tilton and then round up a posse. I can get at least six to start. We'll hunt down that goddamn bear."

"Bad idea," Fargo said, and the man frowned at him. "Any of you experienced bear hunters?" Fargo queried. Carrigan answered with his silence. "A posse tramping around won't get him. He'll avoid you by day and pick you off by night."

"What do you say we ought to do?" Carrigan asked.

"Everyone living around here pull out, leave. No bait, no pickings, and he'll move on away from here," Fargo said.

"And come back God knows when."

"Possibly, but chances are when he sets himself into another territory he'll stay there."

"And if he doesn't?"

"Get yourself a trapper experienced in bear. Let him trap the monster," Fargo said. "That'd be your safest bet."

"That'd take too long. I want to hunt him down now. We can do it," Carrigan insisted.

"I've said my piece. Good luck," Fargo answered and watched the man ride away. Turning the Ovaro south, Fargo went into the valley, passed the Carrigan place, and reached a small cabin. A neat vegetable garden outside lay torn up, half the vegetables eaten, the rest destroyed. He came onto the lower part of the woman's torso, mangled horribly, near the back edge of the vegetable patch. Where others would see only the obvious, Fargo read the signs and marks for all their meanings. The grizzly had lain in wait behind a shed till Amy Baker drew near. Intent on her vegetables, she had perhaps time only to glimpse one huge paw smash her to the ground.

The grizzly had settled down to his bloody pursuits, eating flesh and vegetables at leisure. Fargo moved the Ovaro forward and followed the giant, bloodied paw prints into the forest of box elder and serviceberry. He followed the trail until the place where the bear had entered a deep tangle of loose leaves and vines that made further tracking impossible. He saw that there were other sections of the forest less overgrown as he scanned the woods. The grizzly had chosen the nearest area, a deliberate act to cover his trail. Fargo let a wry sound escape his lips. Carrigan and his amateur hunters would never surprise this grizzly, and Fargo turned his horse back to ride north once again.

The late afternoon shadows stretched over the town when he reached the saloon. Dismounting, he took the rifle from its saddle case, walked into the saloon, and immediately saw there were but a handful of customers in the place. The barkeep had his back to the door as Fargo entered, but he jumped and whirled as the rifle shot exploded, grazed his shoulder, and shattered three whiskey bottles behind the bar. "Jesus," the man said, and his eyes grew wide when he saw Fargo.

"That could've blown your head off," Fargo said and squeezed the trigger again. The rifle shot grazed the bartender's other shoulder and sent glass from three more whiskey bottles flying through the air. "Same with that one," Fargo said.

"Jesus, don't," the bartender said, cringing.

"Why not, you sniveling bastard," Fargo threw back.

"It was Big Jake. He told me to do it," the man said.

"You went along. You took my gun and let the rest happen. You're a piece of shit," Fargo said and raised the rifle. The man cringed again. "I'll take my Colt. Where is it?" Fargo said.

"Right here," the man said and began to reach under the bar.

"Nice and slow" Fargo warned, and the barkeep carefully brought out the gun belt and the Colt in the holster. His hands shaking, he laid everything on the bar and moved back as Fargo stepped up and took the gun belt. Fargo kept the rifle trained on the man as he moved backward across the saloon. The man still had his carbine under the bar, Fargo was certain, and when he reached the door, he continued to back out. But once outside, he didn't make for the Ovaro and the hitching post. Instead, he flattened himself against the wall of the building and waited. The wait took only seconds before the barkeep rushed out, the carbine in his hands, his eyes sweeping the hitching post. Fargo brought the rifle around and smashed it into the man's chubby face. The bartender went down instantly, collapsing in a heap. He was still unconscious as Fargo rode from town in the gathering dusk.

Making a wide circle before returning to Elise, Fargo stopped at Toby's. She came to the door as he dismounted, her eyes on his face and anticipating his words. "I heard," she said and shuddered. "Carrigan was here."

"Leave here. Go visit somebody," Fargo said.

"Can't," Toby answered.

He gave her a derisive glance. "Bull. You want to stay to search for the damn map," he accused, and her shrug was an admission.

"I'll stay locked in and I've the alarm. I'll be fine," she said, stepped forward, and her lips pressed his. "A reminder," she said.

"Don't need one," he said honestly, the picture of her young, firm, round-breasted body flashing through his mind. Her little smile was smug, and he climbed back onto the pinto and heard her bolt the door. He cast a glance at the barn near the house and saw the splintered wood of the sides, the rotten edges where the sides touched the ground. It was a structure in danger of falling down all of itself, he concluded as he rode away, still concerned for Toby's safety.

6

Night had fallen when Fargo reached the Farrell place, and he saw Ernie Walters and one of the other men on guard a dozen yards from the house. He stabled the horse and found Elise had a table set for two and a simple meal waiting. After he finished dinner, she took him into the living room and sat on the sofa beside him, her shallow breasts offering a lovely curve beneath a thin, dark blue bodice. "This was real nice of you," Fargo said.

"I've been waiting for some time to talk to you. How are you holding up?" she asked.

"Another night's sleep and I'll be good as new," he told her.

"The guest room down the hall is waiting for you whenever you're ready. I'll be up late going through an old desk," Elise said.

"Hope the map's there someplace," Fargo said.

Elise leaned closer, and he saw one edge of the long curve of one breast as the garment fell open wider. "You know, I'm no longer sure there is a map," she said, and his brows lifted.

"Seems he talked about a map to a lot of people. You used the word yourself," Fargo said.

"I know, and I also told you it might be no more than a collection of loose notes, references, and cryptic directions. I know Stuart. He enjoyed his own private little jokes, and he enjoyed leading people on," Elise said.

"But you feel there's something," Fargo pressed.

"Yes, I'm sure of that. Either here or . . ." She let the sentence trail off.

"At Amos Cool's place," Fargo finished. Elise's face tightened, and the imperiousness seized hold of her.

"It's entirely possible," she said. "Stu let himself grow entirely too friendly with Amos Cool."

"Man's got a right to choose his friends," Fargo remarked.

"Not when that means leaving his wife almost destitute," Elise said tightly, and Fargo peered at her. She met his eyes and looked away, but with more sadness than anger. "You're surprised by that," she said.

"Yes," he admitted.

"Everyone thought Stu was a wealthy man because he once made a lot of money. They don't know he gambled away most all of it. I reached into what was left to pay you to come here. I expect the balance of what I promised you to come out of what I have when we find the mine. I've also had to set aside the wages for Rick Chowder and the others. There's not much left. That's why I can't have whatever Stuart left fall into anyone else's hands," she said, then paused, her eyes filled with almost desperation as she looked at him. "I know what you're thinking," she said.

"What would that be?"

"That I've more than enough reason to have had Toby Denison knocked out," she said, but all the sharpness was

76

gone from her. Once again, she seemed wounded more than angry.

"The thought came to me," Fargo admitted.

"Only I didn't. It was somebody else. I need the map, or whatever's there, but I have my limits. There are things I wouldn't do," she said, her eyes wide, begging to be believed, and her hands pressed his.

Fargo kept staring at her. If it was a performance, it was a good one, good enough for him to accept, he decided. For now. "I like to take a lady's word," he said, and she leaned to him, her lips on his.

"Thank you," she said. "You won't be sorry."

"Don't figure to be." He smiled and got to his feet. I'll help you clear away."

"No, you go and rest. I'll take care of everything," she said, and he went into the comfortably furnished room, shed clothes, and stretched out in only underdrawers. Sleep still came quickly and deeply to him, and he didn't know how long he had slept when he felt someone shaking him. He forced his eyes open to see Elise standing beside the bed.

"What time is it?" he mumbled.

"Almost morning," she said, and he blinked, took her in more fully, and saw that she had a kerosene lamp on the floor and a roll of parchment in one hand. "I found it," she said excitedly.

"The map?" he said, sitting up.

"No, his notes," she said, waving the roll of parchment. "This is it, I'm convinced, this is all there is."

Fargo rubbed sleep from his eyes and swung long legs around to sit on the edge of the bed. "Let's have a look," he said, and Elise put the lamp atop the dresser where it threw a circle of light. Fargo unrolled the parchment and stared at the collection of scrawled notes, little drawings, and words set down by themselves. "This is going to take time to go into," he said. "Let's leave it till morning."

"All right," she said and put the parchment atop the dresser. She returned to sit down beside him, her eyes moving over his near nakedness. "I'm too excited to sleep," she said, her hand coming to rest on his shoulder.

"Then you need to relax," he said, and her hands moved across his chest as she murmured yes. "You'll need help," he said.

"Yes, oh, God, yes," Elise said softly and he reached a hand up to help her undo the top of the bodice. She wriggled and the garment fell away. He watched her raise long legs and kick away the remainder of her clothes. The longish breasts were shallow, he saw, but exotically lovely, their slow, long concave curves immensely attractive. Each breast lay tipped with a dark red nipple, slightly crinkled at the top, against a wide circle of lighter red. Broad shoulders and a slender rib cage tapered down to a long, narrow waist, her body willowy, belly flat, ribs showing, and a very modest triangle entirely in keeping with her understated loveliness. Slender legs retained enough firmness to keep their curves, altogether a body that looked younger than it was.

She turned to him, and his hand closed around one shallow breast, caressed its softness, and Elise's legs moved, then rubbed against each other, and she gave a tiny sigh. His lips came down to close around one breast and gently pull at the dark red nipple. Her little cry took on new strength and her arms encircled his neck. "Harder," she whispered, "harder." He let his lips answer, and Elise cried out in pleasure, and he felt her legs rubbing against each other again. Suddenly, her hands

78

were swarming all over him, finding him, pulling, caressing, and she half screamed with desire. "Yes, yes, Jesus, let's go, let's go," she cried. "God, I need it, I need you, oh, God yes." He let his hand slide downward onto the modest nap and felt the soft-hard swell of her Venus mound, and her hips lifted, rotated in a half-circle, and then fell back onto the bed again. She uttered a sharp scream as his hand slipped down to the bottom of the triangle and pressed against her.

Again, her hips rose and rotated, and he pressed further in between the slender thighs and felt the moistness already there. "Take me, oh, please, take me, take me, dammit," Elise cried out, sharpness and pleading mingling in her voice. He reached out and caressed the dark, wet entrance, and Elise's slender torso lifted again, shook, fell back, surged up and back, and in her every movement he felt the urging demand. He came over her and rested his own throbbing warmth against the modest nap for a moment. She cried out in anticipation, arms tightening around him, thighs coming in to press tight against him. He slid forward slowly, and Elise uttered a wild yet wailing sound, a cry of wanting and welcome, a paean to passion too long unvisited. Her slender legs rose and folded around his hips, then pressed tight as she surged with his every sliding thrust, met sweet pressure with sweet embrace, sensation matching sensation, ecstasy entwined within itself.

Elise's hips began to rotate again, faster, and now her slender legs were rubbing up and down against his body. Her mouth open, gasping in air and making tiny sounds, Fargo heard her calling his name, over and over, as though it could heighten pleasure by its very sound. She fell into a rhythm that fitted their thrustings, a whispered accompaniment to passion, until suddenly she broke off, moaning replacing his name, rising in pitch as her body began to tremble. "More, more, harder, harder," she said between moans and surged against him violently, again and again until she was shaking and quivering with every thrust, shallow breasts lifting, offering, trembling. He took one, then the other, held them in his mouth and felt her trembling against his tongue, and then, with a wild spasm, she screamed and her body seemed to explode. "Now, now, now, oh, Jesus, now," she screamed, and he felt himself one with her, unable to hold back, caught up in the embrace of all embraces where there was only the ultimate pleasure.

Elise screamed, a shattering, primeval sound, and her slender body vibrated violently, every part of her shaking, shallow breasts falling to one side, then the other. He felt her contract around his throbbing maleness, dark and wet tremblings of their own. But the ultimate finally spiraled beyond ecstasy, and she went limp and pulled him to her, stayed around him, holding him inside her. "Don't go, don't go," she whispered, and he remained in the wonderful embrace, all the residue of passion clinging with soothing stubbornness. Finally, she fell away, slender legs moving from him, arms falling to her sides, and he came to lay half over her. "Why does it have to end so quickly?" she murmured.

"Maybe because we couldn't stand it if it lasted longer," he said. "Not much of an answer, but I don't have a better one."

She nodded and settled down beside him and was asleep in his arms in what seemed seconds. She stayed there with him until the sun of the new day slid into the room. He was awake when she sat up and let him enjoy the concave curve of her breasts before she pulled on her blouse. "It was better than I remember," Elise said.

"Water is especially good when you're dying of thirst," Fargo said.

She smiled. "Yes, I suppose so," she agreed. "But I won't be having that problem now."

"We've a mine to find first," he said.

"Not first, along with," she corrected. "And after you find it, maybe you won't want to move on."

"We'll see," he allowed, and she kissed him, hard and long, to emphasize her message.

"I'll get us some breakfast," Elise said, rising as she finished dressing and pausing at the doorway to look back, a satisfied smile edging her thin lips. "Now I know you'll be concerned only about Toby Denison's safety," she said.

"Never said otherwise," he remarked.

"I never take anything for granted," Elise answered and hurried away. Fargo rose, used the basin and cloth to wash up, dressed, and took the parchment into the living room. Elise had coffee waiting on the table, and he saw her outside talking to Ernie Walters and Rick Chowder. Fargo opened the parchment and weighed the corners down with the cups and candlesticks. He sipped the coffee as he studied the document.

"You're working on it," she said excitedly. "What have you found?"

"Not a lot so far, but it seems to be a kind of guide. Everything has another meaning. Everything refers to something else, but we have to figure out the first meanings," Fargo said.

The parchment was headed by two words scrawled in decisive penmanship fashioned with a broad-tipped quill pen. "Orient Temple," Elise read aloud. "What's that mean?"

"That's probably the simplest thing on here," Fargo said. "What's another name for an oriental temple? Pagoda. That'd mean Pagoda Peak at the western edge of the Shadow Mountains. He's given a very general landmark as a starter."

"We head toward Pagoda Peak then," Elise said.

"In a general way," Fargo said, and he read aloud from the rest of the parchment. "Three nighttime suns. *Hanyewi. Waziyata.*"

"Indian words?" Elise interrupted.

"That's right." Fargo nodded. "Then he goes back to English. Acres of adoration."

"What the hell does that mean?" Elise asked impatiently.

"I'll have to work on that," Fargo said. "Next line he goes back to Indian. *Nut-hi-e.* Then below, the last note is in English. It's a reference, sort of poetic. 'Like a grand lady wearing a cloak of practical reddish brown outside lined with marbled cream and brown inside.' "

"I told you Stu enjoyed playing games with people. He made these purposely cryptic," Elise said.

Fargo rose, finished the last of the coffee, and took the parchment under his arm. "I'm going to have to put my thinking cap on. I'll want to be quiet and alone," he said.

"Of course," Elise said, and Fargo closed the door to the guest room as he went inside with the parchment. He spread the material out again, keeping it flat, and sat down to peer at the words. He'd already deciphered the reference to Pagoda Peak, and he went to the second line . . . "Three nighttime suns." He sat back and let the phrase seep through his mind as he let his thoughts become almost dreamlike, allowing memories, information, long-buried kernels of knowledge, all the accumulation of the Trailsman's lore surface in free association. He forced himself to stay away from the intense concentration that too often blocked the mind from finding its own secrets.

He went from phrase to phrase, word to word, grew angrily impatient with himself again and again, and lost awareness of time. But a good part of the day had passed when he finally rose, satisfied that he had made sense out of the cryptic, esoteric array of words and phrases. Elise came in from the kitchen as he entered the living room, her eyes searching his face. "I wanted to bring you something to eat, but I was afraid to disturb you," she said. "I've a beef sandwich ready."

"I'll take it while we go over what I've got," he said, and she hurried away to return with the sandwich and a bourbon. She sat on the edge of the sofa as he began to reconstruct what he had deciphered, her long fingers curled tightly. "Nighttime suns," Fargo began. "This is a Sioux word he uses, *hanyewi*, though Indians everywhere use the same general term for this. It means moon. They call the moon the nighttime sun, *hanyewi*. Three nighttime suns, he writes. That means we travel for the three suns and three nighttime suns, three days and three nights."

"Starting from here, I imagine," Elise said.

"I'd guess so," Fargo grunted. "The next word he uses, *waziyata*, is also Sioux, but it's harder to pin down. It comes from other Sioux words. According to Sioux mythology, *tate*, the wind, had four sons, *Okaga*, which comes from *itokaga*, the south, *Eya*, which comes from *wiyohpeyata*, the west, *Yanpa*, which comes from *wiyohiyanpa*, the east; and *Yata*, which comes from *Waziy-*

ata, the north. *Yata* is the north son of *tate*, the wind or the north wind. He's giving us a place, in Sioux terms, where the north wind blows, probably constantly."

"Damn his cleverness," Elise bit out.

"The next one, 'acres of adoration,' gave me more of a problem. I wrestled with that one most of the morning, and suddenly it came to me, floated up out of memory by itself. From the time of the ancient Greeks, flowers have been given meanings. Poets, writers, philosophers, and oracles have used these meanings, as well as generations of good ladies in their gardens. A whole body of people have believed in the meaning and the power of flowers, plants, and trees. The bluebell means kindness, the clover industriousness, the daisy innocence, the geranium gentleness, the hyacinth playfulness. There are hundreds more, and I sure as hell don't know most of them, but I finally remembered adoration. The dwarf sunflower means adoration. Not the regular, tall sunflower with its big leaves. That means haughtiness. The dwarf sunflower . . . adoration."

"Acres of adoration," Elise breathed. "Somewhere there are acres of dwarf sunflowers, acres of adoration."

"Bull's-eye," Fargo said and finished the sandwich and bourbon. "He's giving us a trail of clues."

"There's more," she said, and he nodded.

"Nut-hi-e," Fargo said, "another Indian word but this one's Onondaga. The Onondaga speak Iroquois. *Nut-hi-e* is their word for noisy leaf."

"Noisy leaf?" Elise frowned.

"The tree of the noisy leaf," Fargo said, and her eyes widened.

"The quaking aspen," she said.

"Bull's-eye, again," Fargo said. "We have to find a big

stand of quaking aspen." He paused and allowed a wry smile. "The last one gave me the most trouble."

"The grand lady?" Elise offered.

"Wearing a cloak of practical reddish brown outside lined with marble cream and brown inside," Fargo finished. "That stumped me. It was the phrase *grand lady* that finally set me in the right direction. I remembered my mother and her friends used to always refer to trees as grand old ladies. I started to think about what kind of cloak would a tree be wearing."

"Its leaves?"

"Yes, but they wouldn't be reddish brown on one side and marbled cream and brown on the other," Fargo said.

"The bark," Elise said.

"Right, and there's only one tree I know of with that kind of bark, leastways up in these parts, the Douglas fir," Fargo said, putting the parchment down. "This is sure as hell no map."

"But it fits right in with what Stu Farrell would do," Elise said. "I can be ready to leave come morning."

"If we're going to come onto a mine, we'll need equipment to explore, pickaxes, tin pans, shovels, lamps, and dynamite. There's no faster way to find if there's a good vein than with dynamite," Fargo said.

"I've everything. Stu kept all his old mining equipment, including dynamite," Elise said. "I'll have everything ready by morning."

"Good enough. I'll go down and check in on Toby right now," he said and saw Elise's face tighten.

"I don't think that's necessary," she said.

"I'm going to tell her I'll be pulling out and try to convince her to leave while that grizzly's still around," Fargo said. "I'll be back later."

"I'll expect that," she said, and then her face softened. "I'll wait for you." She clung for a moment, her mouth working against his, and a confident little smile touched her lips when she stepped back. He left, saddled the Ovaro, and saw he hadn't much of the day left as he rode south. He cut across two heavily overgrown ridges and had just emerged onto an open road when he saw the Owensboro one-horse farm wagon. Ted Carrigan held the reins, his wife sitting beside him, the two children and some luggage in the back of the wagon. Ted Carrigan's face was tense as Fargo reined to a halt.

"Taking the family to stay with some friends," he said, and Fargo's brows lifted.

"It's time. What made you decide? What about that posse?" Fargo asked.

"The posse's been called off. The grizzly killed two of them during the night. He caught each one of them alone," the man said.

"Amateurs," Fargo grunted. "They paid the price." Ted Carrigan made no reply as he snapped the reins over the horse and drove away. Fargo rode on and reached Toby as night fell, carefully stepping the Ovaro over the alarm. But she heard him and waited in the doorway as he dismounted.

"I know about the posse," she said. "I take it you've come again to tell me to leave."

"That and something else," he said. "I'll be pulling out tomorrow morning." Toby's brows lifted, the mist blue eyes questioning silently.

"Elise found the map?" she asked.

"Not a map. She found Stu Farrell's notes. She's certain that's all he left," Fargo said. "They're a series of clues that ought to lead to the mine." Toby's lips pursed as she turned over thoughts in her mind, but she made no comment. "Which means I won't be looking in anymore. Get out of here or you'll end up like Amos," he said.

"Pretty hard words," she said.

"Truth is often hard," he answered.

She stepped closer. "Can you stay?" she asked.

"No. I'm expected back," he said, and she returned a wry smile.

"I told you there wouldn't be a second time," she said.

"I'm not admitting anything. I'm saying it won't be tonight," he told her, and she made a derisive sound. "Now, are you going to pack a bag and get the hell away from this place?" he bit harshly at her.

"Guess so," she said with a half-pout. "Yes," she clarified as he fixed a narrowed glance on her. "You'd best go. You don't want to keep her highness waiting," she said.

"Don't be sharp-tongued with me, girl. I'm here because I care about what's best for you," he tossed at her. Her half-pout dropped away, and she reached up, her lips finding his, high, round, firm breasts pressing hard into his chest.

"Thanks," she murmured. "You can't blame a girl for being disappointed." She stepped back, mist blue eyes holding on him.

"I'll come looking for you when this is finished," he said. She gave him a half-shrug and watched him as he climbed onto the Ovaro. He heard the door bolt snap shut as he rode away. He made a wide circle through the hackberry. But he neither smelled, heard, nor saw any sign of grizzly, so he rode on. When he reached the Farrell place and unsaddled his horse, he found Elise waiting in a floor-length housedress of light blue with buttons down the front. He half expected questions on his visit to Toby, but there were none. Instead, she came to him, her eyes smoldering.

"Same as last night," she said. "Too excited to sleep."

"Sounds like it calls for the same remedy," he said.

"Only my room," she said, taking his hand and leading him into a large room with a full-sized bed covered with pink sheets. She faced him, and he watched her fingers begin to undo the long row of buttons down the front of the dress. By the time she finished and let it fall from her, he was shedding clothes, and he felt himself responding at once. Elise stood in front of him, almost defiantly showing her body's beauty made of shallow curves and slender loveliness. She stretched arms out, and he dropped the last of his clothes and came to her, half lifting her onto the big bed. She folded herself around him, hands, arms, legs, torso, everything surrounding him, clinging, rubbing, pulling. He responded to her fervor and felt his pulsating hotness against her modest nap, pressing into the swell of her Venus mound.

Once again, she whispered sweet demands of "harder" and "more," and the sounds of her pleasure filled the room as her body engulfed his and they became one, a tangle of flesh and sensations, cries and gasps. Elise seemed even more insatiable than the night before and swept him along with her eager, hungering passion. Only when satisfied exhaustion swept over her, and when he felt its pull, did she fall still and silent, and the room no longer echoed to the cries of unrestricted pleasure. She slept tight against him, the night deepening, and he let sleep embrace him as well.

He woke first with the morning, washed, dressed, and made coffee, which he had almost finished when Elise appeared clothed in black denim and a white shirt. "Rick and the others should be getting everything ready. I gave detailed orders last night," she said, her tone crisp and clipped. He smiled to himself. Authority had replaced softness, and he was again amazed at how thoroughly she could separate her two halves.

"I'm sure the place is still being watched, which means they'll see us leave," Fargo said.

"You expect they'll follow," Elise said.

"I'd count on it," Fargo said. "They've been watching for all this while. They won't turn away now that things are starting to happen."

"Wish I knew who they were," Elise said.

"The one called Big Jake and his cronies. People Stu Farrell talked to over the years. Greedy, no-good, rotten bastards who'd do anything to get hold of a silver mine. It doesn't much matter. All that matters is that they'll be coming after us."

"Can you stop them?" Elise questioned.

"Maybe. The right time, the right place. Maybe." He shrugged.

"I'll expect more than maybe," Elise said sharply, and he returned a nod. "Get your things together. I'll tell Rick we're leaving," she said and hurried away. Fargo saddled the Ovaro, and when he finished, he saw Elise ride up on her gray gelding followed by Rick Chowder and the others leading three loaded pack horses and a small burrow that carried two burlap wrapped packs. "The dynamite?" he asked, nodding toward the burrow.

"Yes. It's well wrapped, and there are four packs of phosphorous matches, too," Elise said. He swung in beside her and headed the procession northeast, skirting the high land of the Shadow Mountains. He set a steady pace in the general direction of Pagoda Peak until at day's end he found a spot to camp beside a half-circle of Rocky Mountain maple. "We ought to post night sentries," he said. "Four-hour shifts. That way everybody gets to sleep some."

"I'll tell Rick you'll be running the show," she said, and he unsaddled the Ovaro and set down with a strip of beef jerky as night descended. Elise came to sit beside him soon after and leaned against his shoulder. The other, soft, warm part of her had returned, and he found himself wondering which part of her was predominant. She glanced up to the half-moon slowly crossing the blue velvet cloth that was the night sky. "Nighttime sun number one," she said.

"Two more to go before we look for the other clues," Fargo said.

"You'll have to find a place we can sneak away before this is over. I can't hold out that long. I'm spoiled already," Elise said.

"You spoil quick," he grunted.

"Your fault," she said, kissed him quickly, and got to her feet. "I'm tired. I'm turning in," she said and hurried to where the gray gelding waited. Fargo rose and moved to where Rick Chowder and the others were sitting together.

"I want sentries, two at a time, four-hour shifts," he said.

"Ernie and I'll take the first shift," Rick Chowder said.

"Set up twenty-five yards apart," Fargo said. "You hear or see anything, come get me." The man nodded, and Fargo returned to his own horse, set out his bedroll, and half undressed, laying his gun belt at his side. He fell asleep quickly and knew he hadn't slept long when he snapped his eyes open and saw that the moon hadn't reached the midnight sky yet. His hand closed around the Colt in the holster as he heard the sound of the footsteps that had awakened him. He sat up and saw one of the other men coming toward him at a half-crouch.

"We've got company," the man whispered, and Fargo got to his feet as he strapped on the gun belt.

"You see or hear?" he questioned.

"Heard a horse whinny, pretty close," the man said.

"Only one?"

"That's right," the man said and followed Fargo from the spot through the maples, then halted as Fargo dropped to one knee. "That way," the man said, pointing to the left. "I figure you expected we'd be followed."

"Not this close. They'd hang back. They've no cause to follow close, not yet," Fargo said and motioned to the other sentry. "You circle left," he said to the man. "You circle right," he ordered the other. "I'll go straight. Slow and easy."

He went forward in a crouch, moving carefully through the wide, lobed leaves, straining his eyes in the shadow light of the half-moon. He had gone perhaps a dozen yards when he heard a commotion to his left and then the sentry's voice. "Over here," the man called out, and Fargo straightened and plunged through the trees to come upon the sentry holding his rifle on a shorter figure. The figure turned as Fargo came up, eyebrows arching over mist blue eyes.

"You!" Fargo exploded. "What the hell are you doing here?"

"Staying away from the grizzly. That's what you told me to do, isn't it?" Toby said calmly.

"Goddamn," Fargo swore and took her by the arm. "Bring her horse," he called back at the sentry as he pushed Toby ahead of him, making no effort to be gentle.

7

"You're hurting my arm," Toby protested.

"Too damn bad," Fargo said, but relaxed his grip and leaned closer to her. "You just being a smart-ass?" he whispered.

"I'm protecting my interests," Toby said as he reached the half-circle, still holding on to her. The commotion had wakened Elise, who stood with hands on her hips as she stared at Fargo and at Toby.

"What's she doing here?" Elise frowned, her eyes going to Fargo. "You tell her to come along?" she asked.

"Hell, no," Fargo said.

"Strictly my idea," Toby said.

Elise's eyes blazed at the younger woman. "Then you can march yourself right out of here," she said.

"It's a free country. I can go wherever I like," Toby said.

"Not by following us around," Elise said.

"I've a right to protect my interests," Toby said.

"That's the second time you've said that," Fargo cut in. Toby took two strides to her horse, fished into the saddlebag, and brought out a piece of paper. She handed it to Elise, almost with a flourish.

"There's enough light to read it," she said, and as Elise

held the piece of paper up to catch the moonlight, Fargo read over her shoulder.

To Whom It May Concern:

By these words, all who read this will know that for all his years of companionship and understanding, my good friend Amos Cool is to receive half of all my worldly possessions when I die. To this end, I set down my hand here and now.

Stuart Farrell
October 10, 1859

While Elise still stared at it, Toby took the letter back and folded it into her pocket. "As I'm Amos's only heir and living relative, that makes half the mine belong to me when it's found," she said.

"Ridiculous," Elise bit out.

"Reality," Toby said. "That's Stuart's signature. You know it is." Elise's furious glare was an answer.

"You're not riding with us or camping with us," Elise hissed.

"Don't want to. I'll just follow along. I want to be on hand to protect my interests," Toby said.

"Get her out of here," Elise snapped at Fargo, and he handed Toby the reins of her horse as he started to push his way back through the trees. He led her back to where she'd been camped before he turned to her.

"Why didn't you tell me you were going to pull a stunt like this?" He frowned.

"You'd have told me not to do it," Toby said, and he had to admit the truth of that.

"You're not the only one following," Fargo told her.

"I figured as much," Toby said.

"Which means you could get yourself in the middle of big trouble," he said, and she shrugged. "You stay close," he ordered. "Maybe I can talk Elise into letting you ride along."

She uttered a disdainful snort. "Fat chance," she said. "But I'll stay close."

"See to it," he said, and her hand stopped him as he started to turn away.

"You're not happy with me," she said.

"Go to the head of the class," he growled.

"I'll make it up to you. Promise," she said, and suddenly her arms were around him, the high, firm breasts pushing hard against him. She stepped away just as suddenly, but her little smile was confidently smug. He walked away, fighting down the urge to stay. He wasn't surprised to see Elise still awake and waiting when he returned.

"What took you so long?" she asked sharply.

"Wanted to make sure she's going to keep her distance," he said and unsaddled the pinto and set out his bedroll. He smiled to himself as Elise spread her blanket nearby, undressed in the trees, and returned in her night-gown. The night deepened quickly and stayed quiet.

Fargo woke with the morning, found a patch of wild cherry for everyone to breakfast on, and set a brisk pace as they rode on. Elise stayed with him, silent and still plainly upset. When they camped for the night, she came to him to put her blanket nearby again. Toby had camped almost within sight, and Elise's eyes peered out through the darkness.

"She's staying too close," Elise said tightly.

"She's not the one to worry about," Fargo said.

"You see any signs of others?" Elise queried.

"No, but they're following. Count on it," Fargo said.

"Don't you think you ought to make sure?" Elise asked.

"Figured to do that tomorrow night," Fargo said.

"I'll come along," Elise said.

"No," Fargo said firmly.

"I could help," she said.

"You know better. There's only one reason you want to come along," he said.

"What's that?" She frowned.

"To make sure I don't stop off at Toby," he said.

"Nonsense," she bristled, but looked away from his eyes.

"Whatever you say. The answer's still no," he said, and she walked to her blanket, leaving a trail of silent anger.

He drew sleep around himself and set another brisk pace when morning came. By the day's end, the tall shape of Pagoda Peak rose high and clear, and as darkness descended, he watched the moon rise. Elise came to stand beside him. "The third nighttime sun," he said. "Tomorrow I start looking for the *waziyata*, the north wind. Right now I'm going to look in on our company."

"Nobody else, promise?" Elise said, lips growing tight. "You can get anything you fancy right here. You've not cause to look elsewhere."

"I'll keep that in mind," Fargo said. She fell silent as he climbed onto the Ovaro and rode away, but he felt her eyes boring into him. He passed Rick Chowder and one of the others already standing guard and eased the horse through the trees. It wasn't hard to find Toby, and she sat up from her blanket as he paused, surprise in her eyes.

"You come visiting?" she asked.

"No, but I'll stop on the way back if you're still awake," he said. She nodded, and he moved on through the trees. He rode for another few hundred yards and then swung from the saddle, left the horse tethered to a low branch, and went on alone. He moved cautiously, eyes sweeping the foliage in the moonlight and came to a halt as he heard the sound of a horse to his left. He followed the sound and dropped to one knee as he saw the figures stretched out on the ground, the horses tied to one side.

Most were asleep, he saw, no guards posted. They felt confident. He stepped closer, carefully, silently, bending low to squint along the ground and began to count the figures. His lips formed the number ten as he came to the last figure, and his mouth was a tight line as he carefully drew back from the scene. More of them than he'd expected, he grunted unhappily, and the grimness stayed with him as he returned to the Ovaro and rode back through the heavy woodland. When he reached the spot where Toby had camped, his eyes widened in surprise. A tall, slender figure waited there, arms folded, Toby sitting on her blanket.

"What are you doing here?" he asked Elise in surprise.

"It's called distrust," Toby answered, a faint smile edging her lips.

Fargo's eyes hardened on Elise. "Guess so," he said.

"I just wanted to be sure," Elise said.

"Thanks for the confidence," Fargo tossed back.

"I'm a realist. Men seldom turn down what's waved in front of them," she said.

"Guess you'd know about that," Toby cut in.

"Shut up," Elise snapped at her.

"You, too," Fargo said and turned to Toby. "You've a six-gun with you?" he asked.

"Amos's Remington," she said.

"Good. Get your things together. You'll be riding with us from now on," he said.

"What?" Elise bit out. "Why?"

"We're badly outnumbered. They'll have ten guns when the time comes. We'll need every gun we can get," Fargo said.

Elise frowned at him. "I don't like this. I don't like it at all," she said.

"You've both got an interest in this. You'd better damn well work together on it," Fargo said.

"She's got no interest in this," Elise said.

"That letter says I do," Toby said, gathering her things.

"I don't care what the damn letter says," Elise flung back.

"You've both got an interest in staying alive, don't you?" Fargo cut in, and both women fell silent. "Then you'd damn well better stand together for now. When they come to get that mine, they won't want either of you alive. Now I don't want to hear any more talk about it."

Toby finished gathering her things and pulled her horse along with her as Fargo led the way back to the camp and called out to the sentries as they neared. He unsaddled the Ovaro, set out his bedroll, and lay down. Toby came to put her blanket down a few feet from him, and he saw Elise put hers down on the other side of him. He closed his eyes with a wry smile and the conclusion that the sooner he found the damn mine the happier he'd be. When morning came, he set an early pace and slowed after an hour to draw up beside Elise as Toby looked on from nearby. "Keep Pagoda Peak in front of you and stay north. I'm going exploring," he said and veered to the left as he rode away. They were in mountain country now, plenty of tall hills and patches of level land separating the succession of ridges and peaks.

He rode with his eyes scanning the terrain as he held his head high, letting the wind blow on his face. The *waziyata*, Stuart Farrell had written down. But it wouldn't be just any north wind, Fargo was certain. It had to be a spot where only the north wind blew. He moved the pinto up narrow mountain paths, most made by goats and antelopes, but he spotted enough signs to tell him that the Crow rode these hills. The noon hour passed, and he had gone west, then paused at a mountain stream to let the pinto refresh itself. When he went on, he stayed west, the distant tower of Pagoda Peak a beacon.

A steep path led him upward and he saw the wooded terrain grow sparse as he reached a sharp rock slope where the path continued upward, threading its way alongside the steep crevices that dropped thousands of feet straight down. The wind came at his face from the west, then shifted to the south, then the north, and back to the west as he went from passage to passage. He reached a small ledge of rock, halted, and his eyes narrowed as he took in a steep passage with a sheer wall of rock at one side and a precipitous drop at the other. The passage led upward in a series of sharp turns, but as he gazed at the small mountain brush that grew out of the top of the rock, he saw their sinewy branches all bent in one direction, north. He felt the inner excitement as he rode closer and felt the north wind pull at his face. He peered closely at the mountain brush up high in the rock wall. The wind pushed their leaves north, but he concentrated at the bottoms of the brush where each stem was bent north from where it emerged from the tiny crevices in the rock.

The wind blew only in one direction up this passage, every stem bent north, the oldest and the youngest. He urged the Ovaro a few feet farther, saw that the passage grew steeper and narrower, and left his sight where it curved sharply to the right. Backing the Ovaro a half-dozen yards down to the stone ledge, he turned the horse and rode up another of the mountain paths to where he found a higher ledge that let him see down the mountainous terrain. It took him almost a half hour before he found the others moving slowly along a wider path through the mountainous terrain, and he sent the pinto downward, picked his way in and out of tree-lined paths, and finally emerged in front of Elise and the others.

"The north wind." He saw the excitement leap into her eyes. "Follow me," he said and led the procession back down and finally up to the stone area and halted on the ledge. Toby came alongside Elise as Fargo gestured to the beginning of the narrow, steep passage.

"This one of the clues?" Toby asked, and he caught the disdain in her voice.

"That's right," Fargo said, and the disdain in her voice went into her eyes.

"I don't fancy going up it, that's for sure," she said.

"Can't say I do, but that's where we're going," he said.

"You don't know how far it goes or if we can even go the whole way," Toby protested.

"I expected he wouldn't have given a clue we couldn't use," Fargo said, and his eyes went to the narrow ledge with the sheer drop at one side. He turned to Rick Chowder, who held the reins of one of the packhorses. "Single file and real slow. Bring the mule up at the rear," Fargo ordered. "I'll take the lead."

"I'll go behind you," Elise said, and Fargo saw Toby swing in behind her.

"Anybody's horse gets nervous, you stop and call out," Fargo said. The others nodded, and he turned the Ovaro up the narrow passage, letting the horse walk at its own pace. The north wind immediately blew at his back, sweeping up the passage as if silently calling its own message. He negotiated a slow curve and glanced back. Elise followed some six or seven feet behind, Toby riding at her heels, and Fargo went on. A straight path followed the curve, but remained narrow, and he let the Ovaro continue to set its own pace. The next curve came up, sharp and sudden, and he turned the horse into it to see another equally sharp curve following. Elise and the others were no longer in his view as he glanced back and turned into the second curve, and he forced himself not to urge the pinto on.

The narrow passage continued to be a series of sharp and dangerous curves, and with instinctive horse sense the Ovaro hugged the rock side of the narrow space. Fargo had gone another dozen feet when the scream and the commotion came from his rear, both sounds simultaneous that included the frightened whinny of a horse. Fargo spun in the saddle, but whatever happened had taken place around the second curve and beyond his vision. Another scream, not as sharp, reverberated off the rock wall, and Fargo cursed as he carefully slid from the saddle. "Stay," he murmured to the Ovaro. "Stay. Easy, now, easy." Pressing hands soothingly against the horse's neck, he slid his feet along the few inches of space still left alongside the pinto. The scream came again, then a curse, definitely Elise's voice, and Fargo hurried as he reached the rear of the Ovaro and had more space on the ledge.

He rounded the curve and almost ran into Elise's gray gelding, glimpsed Toby in the saddle directly behind, and heard Elise's cry. Moving carefully past the horse, he peered over the edge of the passage and saw Elise below, precariously balanced on a small rock protrusion some ten feet below. "Jesus, help me," she screamed. "I can't hold on much longer." The protrusion was not more than three feet long and three feet wide, he saw, with only the edges of rock for her to curl her fingers around. He glanced back and saw Rick Chowder had halted at the start of the curve behind Toby, fear in his face.

"Nobody moves," Fargo called out. "Keep your horses calm." His eyes went to Toby as he straightened up and began to walk around the curve to the Ovaro. "I'll get to you later," he muttered, and once again carefully slid his way along the few inches of ledge left alongside the pinto.

"Please," he heard Elise cry, her voice torn with terror. "I'm slipping." He cursed as he took the lariat from its place on the saddle and began to edge his way back to the spot where Elise lay atop the protrusion. He knelt down beside the gelding and cursed the few inches of space he had in which to work. Taking the lariat's loop, he held his arm out as far as he could reach and dropped the rope down along the side of the rock. It landed atop Elise's huddled form, hitting her on the head.

"Pull it down over your shoulders," Fargo called to her.

"I'll fall off if I let go of the rock," Elise said.

"Wait," Fargo said and scuttled himself backward, crab-fashion, until he lay prone, stretched out on the narrow ledge, but still able to look down at Elise. He glanced back at himself, at the narrow space on the ledge, his lips a tight line as he made a final calculation before looking down at Elise again. "Listen to me," he called to her, his voice calm. "Let go of the rock," he said.

"I'll fall," she said, despair and protest curling in her voice.

"I know," he said. "Let go of the rock and pull the loop around your shoulders and under your arms. Do it in one quick motion. Don't try to stop yourself from falling." He saw her look up at him, eyes wide with terror. "Do it," he said quietly, "now." His every muscle tensed as he saw her fingers open, and then she had hold of the lariat half atop her, pulling it over her and under her shoulders, and then she was screaming as she fell from the tiny perch. She plummeted downward screaming, but Fargo yanked hard on the loop, felt it tighten around her, then catch under her arms. He cursed as the impact pulled him forward with a rush, but he was ready, and he spun his body in a half-circle, used his legs to half whirl, and felt the lariat press hard against the edge of the rock ledge.

But Elise had stopped plummeting, and, his shoulder muscles bulging, he hung onto the lariat. Finally, he began to let it play out a little and heard Elise's cry of alarm. Letting the rope out, he again scuttled backward until he was beside the gelding. Without a tree or branch or something to brace himself against, he knew he hadn't the leverage to pull Elise up. Back muscles straining, he managed to straighten up, the rope digging into his hands with her weight at the other end. He gave himself a little more play with the rope and curled it around the saddle horn, took another turn, and one more to be certain. The gelding made nervous little steps, but he soothed it, stroking its neck as he climbed into the saddle.

Ever so gently, he urged the horse forward as he watched the lariat rub against the edge of the cliff. But the rope began to pull upward, and he took another turn of it around the horn and then upward. He let the horse stop to calm itself and pulled on the rope with all the strength of back and shoulder muscles. Elise's short black hair appeared over the top of the passage, and he secured the rope on the saddle horn, slid from the horse, and took the half-dozen steps back to where Elise was trying to pull herself up over the cliff edge. He dropped to his knees, caught her by the arms, and pulled her up onto the ledge. "Oh, God, oh my God," she gasped, and he took the rope from around her. He let her stay there until her breath returned and then helped her to her feet. His eyes went to Toby, who sat motionless on her horse. "You didn't ask for help," she said.

"I know. There was no room for help," Fargo said.

"It was her own fault," Toby's said as Fargo started to gather up the lariat. "She backed up to knock me off the edge, but she lost her balance and went over herself."

"Lying bitch," Elise spit out. "She hit me from behind and knocked me off the horse."

"Bullshit," Toby snapped back.

"That's enough," Fargo cut in. "No more from either of you."

"I'm not riding in front of her," Elise said. "I'm not giving her another chance to kill me."

"I'm not giving her another chance to back into me," Toby said.

"You stay right behind me," Fargo said to Elise. "You stay back six feet," he told Toby and walked around the sharp curve to where the Ovaro waited. Elise nudged the gray up behind him as he climbed onto the horse, and he continued on along the narrow, dangerous passage. The steep-sided ledge moved further upward, remaining a treacherous and delicate passage of sharp twists until it finally widened and leveled off, and Fargo saw a high mountain plateau, densely foliaged, spread out in front of him. The sun was beginning to slide below the distant high peaks, and Fargo waited to let the other catch up. He surveyed Elise and Toby, his eyes narrowed, Elise's face tight and full of icy anger, Toby's a mask of dark, implacable fury. One of them had lied, but he knew neither one was about to admit guilt.

Elise had the most to gain by getting rid of Toby. Yet if Elise were out of the way, Toby could lay claim to the entire mine. He swore silently and decided he'd not waste time trying to decide the truth of what had happened. Preventing another incident was the best he could hope for, and he surveyed both women with a hard stare. "I'm not going to try to find out who tried to kill who," he said.

"Don't you care?" Toby cut in, frowning at him.

"At this moment, not a hell of a lot," he said and saw her lips push out in disappointment. "You want to fight, you'll get plenty of chance in a few days. Meanwhile, any more of this and I walk."

"You've an agreement," Elise said. "You don't back out on agreements. You're not the kind to do that."

"I'll make an exception," Fargo said, and both women fell silent. "Ride," he barked and sent the Ovaro forward across the high plateau that was thick with soft witchgrass and foot-high chickweed. Night came quickly, and he picked a place to bed down where a stand of Rocky Mountain maple clustered in the center of the plateau. Everyone ate in silence, and Rick Chowder came to him when the meal was finished.

"Still want sentries?" he asked. "They probably won't try going through that passage till daylight tomorrow."

"Probably not," Fargo agreed. "All right, no sentries tonight, but back to four-hour shifts tomorrow night." The man nodded and returned to Ernie Walters and the others. Fargo set out his bedroll. Toby appeared with her blanket soon after he was stretched out, and Elise with hers seconds after. Elise could be two very different people, he had learned, and Toby had a brooding stubbornness to her. Yet it was difficult to think of either as a killer, he pondered. But one of them had tried to kill the other; he grunted and realized how hard it was to know people. He'd learned that often enough, yet he never stopped being surprised when he learned it again. He pushed away the grim thoughts, drew sleep around himself, and let the night push away the world.

He was awake and dressed before any of the others when morning came, his gaze searching the high plateau. It ran in a fairly narrow stretch, farther than the eye could see, and beyond it the high country rose up, but less sharply than it had before. Rolling hills reached upward and in the distance became steep mountainsides. Far beyond, the towering top of Pagoda Peak still beckoned. "Stay on the plateau, head toward the peak," he told Elise when she was dressed and ready to ride. "I'll come back to you."

He saw Toby's eyes on him as he rode away and marveled at how she could manage to look disapproving and hurt at the same time. He held the pinto to a canter as he began to explore, his gaze carefully sweeping the wealth of floral growth the plateau harbored. He passed thousands of yards of the pale violet leaves and white flowers of Colorado blue columbine, more of the russet buds and green stems of rosecrown, and even more of the green-flecked, pale yellow arctic gentian that seemed determined to imitate the lily. He sent the horse from one side of the plateau to the other, and finally, as he neared the end, he turned into a forest of white balsam. He pushed his way through the cone-shaped conifers, enjoying the wonderful fragrance that surrounded him. The day had begun to slide toward its end, and he was growing frustrated when the stand of balsams suddenly stopped, and he rode out onto another flat stretch of high land. But this time he uttered a grunt of satisfaction.

A carpet of dwarf sunflowers blanketed the land, their yellow-orange flowers with their slightly darker centers standing out boldly against their bright green somewhat heart-shaped leaves. He turned the Ovaro and hurried back through the balsam to meet the others as they came up along the plateau, Elise in the lead, Rick Chowder with her, Toby riding off by herself. Everyone turned as they saw him and followed him back through the trees to the vast field of the dwarf sunflowers.

"Acres and acres of adoration," Elise breathed, her eyes filled with excitement.

"The dwarf sunflower means adoration," Fargo said to Toby as he saw her perplexed frown.

"Another of his clues?" Toby asked, her frown staying.

"The fourth one," Fargo said, and she gave a disdainful snort. He peered at her, but she said nothing more, so he turned away.

"It'll be dark before we reach the end of the sunflowers. We'll camp here in the balsams and go on come morning," Fargo said.

"I'm really excited. We're getting closer," Elise said, and Fargo glanced at Toby. Her expression was fixed, almost a sneer, he saw as he led the Ovaro to a small clearing in the balsams. He set out his bedroll, and night fell as he finished his strip of beef jerky when Toby appeared before him, and he saw the annoyance in her face as she regarded him.

"You've a burr under your saddle," Fargo said.

"This is a wild-goose chase. All those crazy clues don't mean anything," she said.

"Stuart Farrell wrote them out. Of course they mean something," Fargo said.

"Not for the mine," she said adamantly. "He left a map, not a list of crazy clues."

"You sound awfully sure of that. Why?"

"He told Amos often enough. He left a map, someplace, somewhere," Toby insisted.

"If you're so sure, why'd you follow along?" Fargo asked.

"I thought she'd found something more. I decided to go see, just in case," Toby said.

"Why don't you go back, then?" Fargo questioned.

"I've come this far. I'm curious where this'll lead. Maybe it will lead somewhere." She shrugged. When he said nothing more, she turned and strode way. Fargo undressed and lay down on the bedroll, put hands behind his head, and waited. It took a longer time than usual, but the figure finally appeared, holding a blanket, took form as Elise, and he watched her set her blanket down near him. He lay awake and found himself growing surprised when Toby didn't appear to set down her blanket. He rose, finally, and saw Elise sit up at once, her breasts partly revealed in their lovely, long curve as her nightdress dipped low. He knew she watched him as he walked from the bedroll, clad only in undershorts. Walking quickly, he surveyed the area, saw the two men asleep, and then spied the blanket beside a sapling, Toby half wrapped in it.

Elise was still sitting up when he returned to his bedroll. "You went looking for her," she said tersely. "You thought something had happened to her."

"It crossed my mind," he said, sinking down on his bedroll.

"What if she'd come with her blanket, and I'd stayed away? Would you have come looking for me?" Elise questioned.

"Count on it," Fargo said. Elise lay back on her blanket as he stretched out.

"Thank you," she murmured, her voice suddenly soft. "That makes me feel much better."

"Get to sleep," he said, refusing to be drawn in further, but when he closed his eyes, he felt her hand touch his, stay there, and press harder. Her voice followed, a whisper.

"Make love to me, Fargo," she said.

"When this is over, maybe," he said. She stayed silent and finally drew her hand away.

He turned on his side and slept until the morning sun woke him. He found a small stream where everyone refilled canteens and watered the horses before he led the way forward. Elise rode at his right, and Toby came up to ride at his left, and he noticed the faint air of disdain still clung to her face. It was near midday when the fields of sunflowers came to an end, and Fargo saw the plateau begin to rise, changing to sloping terrain that swept upward. A quick glance at the distant tip of Pagoda Peak told him the acres of sunflowers had led them west, and he held to the course as he led the others west up the sloping terrain. Elise and Toby had fallen behind him, but he saw they kept plenty of room between them.

The terrain continued to rise, and he had led the way to a pond by midafternoon where the others rested and watered the horses while he went on another five hundred yards. A wind had come up, and he heard the unmistakable sound before he saw the trees, and then he came onto them, a long, dense stand of quaking aspen. He halted and listened to the distinctive shimmering, quivering sound made only by one tree, the "noisy leaf" of the quaking aspen. He returned to the others and led them along the aspen forest until night began to descend. The aspen still gave voice as dark fell, and he camped in the midst of their rustling lullaby. Toby paused beside him when he'd finished eating, the faint disdain still in her eyes. "How many more of these clues?" she asked.

"One more," he said.

"Thank God," she said brusquely.

He studied her for a moment. "What if all this leads to the mine?" he asked.

"I'll be real surprised," she said.

"You going to apologize then for all this sarcasm?" he asked.

"You going to apologize for not believing me at the cliff?" she shot back, and the frown dug into his brow. Was she really as hurt as she sounded? That would say something. Or was she just being clever? That would say something, also. He wasn't ready to desert caution, he decided.

"That depends," he answered.

"What happened to looking out for me?" Toby muttered.

"It's on hold," he said, and she gave a snort as she turned on her heel and stalked away. He lay down on his bedroll, and minutes later Elise brought her blanket and set it down close to him.

"We're getting close. I can feel it. I'm excited," she said. "Aren't you?"

"I'll get excited when it's over," he said.

"I'm counting on that, too," Elise said, and her hand came out to close over his. He fell asleep with her hand over his, and when morning came, he rose, looked over to see her on her side, one long, slender leg almost totally exposed, and he found he had to stop himself from lying down beside her. He gathered his bedroll, washed with the water from his canteen, and saw Toby awake, just buttoning her shirt as he approached. Her mist blue eyes clouded instantly with reproach when she saw him. With an air of defiance she stopped buttoning her shirt and let most of the firm, very round, high breasts stay exposed.

"Very nice," he commented as he walked by. "Maybe some other time."

"It wasn't an offer," she said, and he questioned with a glance. "Just a reminder," she finished tartly.

"Didn't need one," he said and went on to saddle the Ovaro. When the others were ready, he led the way through the aspen, and when the forest ended, he saw a wide slope that led upward and still to the west of Pagoda Peak. Halfway up the slope, the stand of Douglas fir beckoned, the very tall, thin trunks topped by the unmistakable conical, compact crowns. He waved the others forward as he rode into the forest of the giant trees, many towering over two hundred feet in height. The forest made a slow half-circle westward up the slope, and he followed its path, pausing only to give the others a chance to catch up with the heavily loaded packhorses. The day had moved into midafternoon when he saw the forest beginning to thin out, and when he rode out of the last of the giant firs, he halted. His eyes moved up another slope, this one less steep, the land more open and bordered by short, stout clusters of Rocky Mountain juniper.

As the others arrived and caught sight of him, he moved forward up the wide slope, and as he neared the top, he saw the shapes take form, small wooden sheds and the open mouths of four mine shafts. He drew up to where the mine shaft openings were clustered in a half-circle, some twenty-five yards apart, heavy wood beams erected atop and around the entrance to each mine. He dismounted and scanned a residue of half-rusted tin pans and broken shovels that lay around the site. Elise was first to ride up, then Rick Chowder and one of the pack-horses. Toby followed him, brought her horse near Fargo, and dismounted. She frowned as she swept the scene with a slow glance.

"There's no secret, hidden mine here. Those are all old abandoned mine shafts," she said, frowning.

"It looks that way, but Stuart obviously knew better. He knew there was silver here," Elise said.

Toby gave a derisive snort. "This is a laugh. There's nothing here," she said.

"Of course there is. We'll check each mine shaft. You'll see," Elise said.

"Crap," Toby spit out. "You've been following some old notes he put down about how to get to this place God knows how long ago." Fargo felt his own frown as he scanned the scene.

"No, you're wrong," Elise insisted and turned to Fargo. "Don't listen to her. We'll check each mine shaft. One of them will be a strike. You read Stuart's notes yourself. They were written to keep this place hidden."

"It seems that way, yet they could've been set down long ago, before he checked out this place and then abandoned it. I don't know," Fargo admitted.

"I know," Toby said, disgust in her voice.

"This has to be it, I tell you," Elise said angrily.

"I know one thing. That's exactly what Big Jake and his friends are going to think," Fargo cut in. "They'll figure this is it, and they'll attack come morning. They'll do their own searching and finding after they've gotten rid of us."

"We expected they'd come at us. Now we've got to stop them," Elise said.

"I'm not for getting myself killed over some worthless mines," Toby sniffed.

"Then get the hell out of here," Elise flung at her. "We don't need you."

"Yes, we do," Fargo cut in and turned to Toby. "You can't run. They know you're with us. They'll go after you. They'll hunt you down. You came along to protect your interests. Your words. Now you'll have to protect your neck."

The bitter anger in her eyes told him she realized the hard reality of his words, and he cast a glimpse at the sky. "It'll be dark in half an hour," Elise said, following his eyes.

"I'm going to do some checking. When I get back, we'll make plans. Meanwhile, take the horses away from the mine shafts. Tether them back by that stand of junipers," Fargo said and swung onto the pinto. He rode quickly down the slope and reached the edge of the firs just as he glimpsed two figures emerging from the forest. He sent the pinto into the trees and watched the two riders dismount and creep up the slope on foot as darkness descended. They dismounted and vanished from view in the dark, but he waited, and after a spell they came back down the slope, climbed onto their horses, and went into the forest. They'd seen the mine shafts and were on their way to carry the news to the others. Fargo followed on foot and halted when they rejoined the others, where the moonlight let him see Big Jake's monstrous shape amid the other figures.

He also saw something else. Each man had two rifles. He silently cursed at the meaning of that. They had come prepared to switch rifles instead of taking the time to reload, a maneuver that would let them lay down a blanketing barrage of gunfire. Fargo watched them begin to settle down for the night and carefully moved away through the firs. His thoughts were already racing to make plans as he rode back on the Ovaro, one thought dominating all others: They were outnumbered and outgunned. They were as good as dead unless he could find a way to overcome the odds.

8

Fargo saw the faint pink of dawn touch the sky as he peered up from inside the mine shaft. He crouched just inside the entranceway in the largest of the shafts. Beside him, Elise stirred, and he put a finger to his lips. Blackness still stayed inside most of the mine shaft. They had all argued with him when he'd returned, all except Toby. She listened, taking no part and wrapping herself in an air of detached resignation.

Rick Chowder had been the first to make suggestions after listening to what Fargo had said. "They'll have to move up at us. We lay low and pick them off as they come," he had said.

"No good," Fargo had answered. "Soon as we start shooting, they'll know where we are. They're ready to lay down a barrage that'll wipe us all out."

"Then we move up the mountainside and take up positions," Elise had put in.

"They'll like that. They know we'll have to come down sooner or later. They'll just dig in and wait," Fargo had said. "We can't fight them in the open. They're too strong. We've got to surprise them."

"How?" Rick Chowder had asked.

"From inside the mine shafts," Fargo said and drew a murmur of protest from everyone except Toby.

"We'll be trapped inside. We'll have to come out, and they'll be waiting there to slaughter us," Chowder said.

"For what I have in mind, I want them waiting for us. I want them taking up positions at each shaft," Fargo said and almost smiled at the collective frowns that faced him. He had carefully given them his plan, the only plan with any chance of victory, and the time to put that plan into action was suddenly upon them. Elise had insisted she go with him, and he'd sent Toby into one of the other shafts with Rick Chowder. The other three men were closeted in the third shaft, and now Fargo watched the day grow stronger and begin to seep into the mine. He rose and reached over to the three sticks of dynamite beside him and felt Elise press against him.

He inclined his head, straining his ears to pick up sounds from outside the shaft. They came, finally, horses moving carefully past the four mine shafts. He waited, his lips a tight, thin line. They were moving up the slope, spread out, checking to find their quarry, and Fargo waited. Those in the other shafts would wait to take their cue from him. Now the sun had come up to send a narrow ray of yellow probing into the mine.

Fargo stepped back from it to stay in the shadows, pushing Elise with him. It wasn't longer than another ten minutes when Fargo heard the hoofbeats returning, then the sounds of the men dismounting.

He listened to them take up positions in front of the mine shaft and knew they were doing the same at the other shafts. It was Big Jake's voice that shouted, a gruff bellow. "We know you're down there. You're dumber than we figured," the voice called, waited, and getting no answer, called out again. "You come on out now, and we can make a peaceable agreement," the man said, attempting to coat his gruffness with reasonableness. Fargo motioned to Elise, and she struck one of the sulphur-tipped matches and handed it to him. He lit the fuse on the dynamite stick, counted silently to ten, then heaved the stick out of the mine entrance. He watched it arc into the air until it disappeared out of his line of vision. But he heard Big Jake's voice. "What the hell . . . ?" the man snapped, and then, realization coming to him, "Jesus, look out!"

The stick of dynamite exploded, a deafening blast, and Fargo could feel the shock waves reaching back into the mine shaft. Shouts and curses were quickly drowned out when two more explosions followed from two of the other mine shafts. Fargo had another stick of dynamite lighted, and he threw it out of the mouth of the mine, listened to it explode with a ground-shaking roar, and then started out of the mine. The Colt in hand, he swung up the few rungs of the entranceway ladder, reached the mouth of the mine, and instantly dropped to one knee as his eyes swept the scene.

Four of the attackers lay scattered and lifeless, but he saw three more flattened on the ground as they fired their rifles as best they could at the figures that emerged from the other mine shafts. One of Rick Chowder's men went down, and Fargo dived to the ground as bullets tore into the mine shaft timbers directly behind him. He rolled, flattened himself on his stomach, and drew a bead on the nearest attacker. He fired, and the man's body jerked, then lay still as the rifle fell from his hands. Fargo's eyes moved across the slope as the others continued to exchange fire, and he spotted the huge form in the distance, just reaching the edge of the line of junipers that edged the slope. Pushing to his feet, Fargo ran, staying in a crouch, aware that behind him the shots still sounded, though they had dwindled down to a sporadic exchange. He stayed in the crouch until he reached the trees where he spotted the bulky form pushing through the foliage.

Big Jake had decided the smart thing was to flee, and Fargo went forward, staying to one side as he closed distance. The lumbering figure suddenly stopped and turned toward him. Fargo threw himself into a headlong dive as a volley of shots exploded, and he heard the bullets crashing through the trees on both sides of him. Big Jake was furiously firing two guns, Fargo realized, and he stayed flattened on the ground, unmoving, until the shots abruptly ended. Big Jake had paused to reload, and Fargo lifted himself to his feet and darted a half-dozen feet to hunker down behind the trunk of an old juniper. He peered around the fibrous bark and saw the mountainous bulk moving again, staying low. Fargo raised the Colt and fired, the single shot crackling through the trees, followed by the thudding sound of Big Jake's body crashing to the ground.

Fargo straightened, his gaze on the big bulk lying amid the trees and brush, looking not unlike a mound of earth in the forest. He holstered the Colt, stepped to Big Jake, and started to push the huge mound of flesh with the point of his foot when, with astonishing speed, the huge bulk exploded. Big Jake swung one huge arm out and smashed it into Fargo at the ankles. Fargo felt himself topple forward and Big Jake's knee catch him in the ribs. He fell sideways, rolled, and came up on his back to see Big Jake bringing his two guns up to fire. Fargo yanked the Colt free of its holster and fired from the hip as he lay on his back. His five shots all struck home, and the mountainous bulk quivered, its fat shaking as the bullets thudded into it. Slowly, still vibrating, the huge form sank to the ground, quivered for the last time, then lay still.

Fargo pushed to his feet and let a long sigh escape him as he reloaded and walked from the junipers. As he stepped from the trees, his eyes swept the open land in front of the mine shafts. He saw Elise, Toby, Rick Chowder, and Ernie Walters. They were the only ones standing, the ground littered with still forms in the grotesque positions of the lifeless. "The dynamite did it," Elise said as he reached her. "It took out most of them right away."

"They still got Roy and Charlie," Rick Chowder said.

"They'd have gotten all of us if they hadn't been so dazed they couldn't really concentrate their fire," Elise said.

"Big Jake got away," Chowder said.

"He tried to," Fargo said tightly.

"What now?" Toby asked.

"We start exploring each mine," Elise said.

"After we clear away all these bodies," Chowder said.

"Drag them all to the edge of the junipers. We'll bury them in one of the mines after we're done searching," Fargo said and joined with Chowder and Walters for the grim task. There was still most of the day left when they finished, and the packhorses were brought down, the equipment unloaded—kerosene lamps, pickaxes in various sizes, shovels, small hand picks, and stacks of tin pans. "We start with the two smaller mines," Fargo said to Elise. "You go with Rick and Ernie in one. I'll take the other."

"Fine," she said and began to pick up the tools and lamps. Fargo cast a glance at Toby.

"You going to help?" he tossed at her.

"Why not?" she said with a shrug and took up one of the kerosene lamps and followed him as he walked to the next mine entrance. She put the lamp on as he climbed down into the mine and followed as he halted at the first level some fifteen feet down. A small platform of timbers had been erected, and Toby set the lamp down where he could see to attack the dirt and stone walls. She used a small hand pick as he swung a large double-ended pick to dig into the wall. She continued her truculent silence, and after some hours he moved down deeper into the mine and Toby followed. He chipped and pounded and dug into the dirt and stone sides of the mine shaft, pausing frequently to search what he'd dug for the telltale silvery blue that marked the precious ore. When the pain in his arms and back told him the hours had gone round too long, he quit and climbed up the shaft with Toby at his heels.

It was dark when they came out of the mine, except for the burning kerosene lamps in a half-circle. Elise waited with Rick and Ernie nearby, and he had only to see the mixture of disappointment and defiance in her face. "No luck in this one, either," he said.

"It'll be one of the next two," she said, and he heard the forced confidence in her voice.

"Get a good night's sleep. I know everybody's tired. We'll start again come morning," he said, walked away, and took his bedroll halfway up the slope. Elise came up soon after, lay down on her blanket, and was asleep in seconds. His throat felt dry, and he rose to go the canteen that lay attached to the saddle alongside the Ovaro. He passed Toby on the way and saw she was sitting up, still awake. Her blouse hung open, and he could see the lovely, high, very round breasts. She glanced at him, and he saw the taunting in her eyes. "Don't say it," he growled.

"Not yet," she said smugly and made no effort to pull the blouse closed.

"You saying something?" he asked.

"You apologizing?" she tossed back.

"Not yet," he said, and she turned her back to him and lay down. He moved on to his bedroll, lay down, and embraced the soothing touch of sleep. The morning sun had risen above the distant peaks when he rose, and he was still the first to wake. He'd finished washing and was dressed when the others stirred and rose, and when they were ready to return to the mines, he took the largest of the two remaining shafts. Once again, Toby followed him down the ladder just inside the mouth of the mine, and once inside, Fargo quickly saw that the mine went deeper than any of the others with more wooden work platforms and many more timbers needed to shore up the walls. "Let's go down as far as we can before we start digging," he said to Toby and took the lamp as he began to climb downward on the ladders that were built vertically along the shaft walls.

He finally halted where the shoring timbers came to an end and examined the walls. It was obvious that the mine had been worked, the gouges and marks deep into the dirt and rock. Raising the big pickaxe, he plunged it hard into the nearest wall and began to dig. Toby alternated between a small hand pick and a shovel as she worked alongside him and he made deep cuts and carved a circle that touched every part of the walls. He went down deeper, as far as the timbers would permit, dug and cut and gouged again, and finally climbed upward to the next platform. He kept up the hard and painstaking exploration and allowed only a few moments of rest before going to the next level. Fargo felt the grimness settling over him as the hours went by, and Toby worked beside him without a word. Finally, they came to the top platform where a glimmer of daylight normally seeped through, and he saw that the day had ended and only the darkness of night filtered into the shaft.

He finished digging, his back and arms pulsing with pain. They had dug nothing but rock and dirt, useless shale, and a few strains of pyrite and gypsum. Toby let him help her up the last few steps of the ladder. Outside, she sank down to the ground, exhaustion etched on her face. Her perspiration-soaked blouse outlined every curve of her breasts, and her loveliness seemed an intrusion in this moment of painful truth. He turned away to focus on Elise, who waited with her face tight, the two men in the background.

"There's no silver in that mine," Fargo told her with more brusqueness than he intended. "If there ever was silver here, it's been long gone. These shafts are all mined out."

"But the clues, everything he put down that led us here," Elise said. "Why? What did it mean?"

Fargo's expression held discomfort. "It meant he put it all down when he first found his place. He was keeping it a secret then, and he obviously put down the clues to help himself find it again and keep others from finding it. God knows how long ago that was, but he came back since then and worked the mines for whatever they had. Toby was right about this."

"Thanks for nothing," Elise spit out, turned on her heel, and walked away. Fargo saw Toby push to her feet, a wry smile on her face.

"I was right about more than this," she muttered to Fargo. "He left a map. It's someplace."

"Maybe it was all talk," Fargo said. "And if it wasn't, maybe it's just not around anymore."

"Maybe," Toby said. "Anyway, I'm cutting out. I'm going back."

He peered at her. "You're going back to look for the map again," he said.

"Maybe," she said.

"You forget about that grizzly?" Fargo asked.

"He's probably gone his way," Toby said.

"I wouldn't count on it," Fargo said.

Her brows arched as she fastened him with a gaze that was part cool condescension and part resentment. "Why the concern for somebody who attempted murder?" she slid at him.

"I never said that. I said I'd no way of knowing who was responsible on that ledge. That's not the same as accusing someone," he answered.

"It is to me." She sniffed, her eyes flashing. He watched her go to her horse and begin to pack her things. He still didn't know what had happened on the ledge, he realized, but her adamant, hurt anger almost demanded believing. He waited till she'd finished fastening her saddlebags before he went to her.

"How are you going back?" he questioned.

"The way we came," she said.

"You could wait till morning to start back," he said.

"I'll enjoy my own company better. I'll find a spot to bed down," she said.

124

"I'll come pay you a visit," he said, offering an olive branch.

"There's no need," she said stiffly, climbing into the saddle. "Don't do me any favors."

"Maybe I want to," he said. She refused to answer and sent her horse into a trot as she rode away. He turned and walked back to see Elise had set her blanket out near the edge of the junipers. Her eyes were cold as she watched him approach.

"I thought you were going to kiss her good-bye," Elise snapped, her voice heavy with sarcasm.

"Didn't figure to," Fargo said blandly.

"Good riddance, I say," Elise grunted.

"What do you plan on doing now?" Fargo questioned.

"We've dynamite left. I told Rick we should do some blasting," Elise said.

"I'm convinced it won't do any good. I didn't see even a hint of silver. These mines are played out," Fargo said.

"I want to try further," she insisted.

"Your call, but I'll be heading out in the morning," he said and saw her eyes widen.

"You can't do that. I need you. Maybe I'll find another map," she said.

"More likely you won't," he said. "And if you do, God knows when."

"You can't go. You didn't find the mine. That was our agreement," Elise said.

Fargo frowned. "I deciphered what you found and brought you here. That filled my part of the agreement," he said. "I'm done. I'll be taking the rest of my fee."

Elise's lips tightened. "I can't give it to you," she said, and Fargo's frown deepened. "I told you I was almost out of money. I can't just give over that much now."

"You made the agreement," Fargo said.

"I expected to pay you out of the silver we found," she said. Her arms went around his neck. "Stay, work with me on this. You'll get every bit of your fee and a lot more. I promise."

"I'm sure you'll try, but I'm finished. I don't think there's a map. Toby was right. This is all a wild-goose chase. We made an agreement, and I expect you to keep it," he said.

She pulled her arms down and stepped back. "Will you sleep on it? That's not too much to ask," she said, suddenly all soft pleading with the way she could switch personalities.

"I guess not," he agreed.

"I'll be right back. I told Rick and Ernie we'd be searching again, but if you leave, I'll probably give up. I want to tell them maybe we won't be going on. That's only fair," she said.

"I suppose so." He nodded and sat down on the blanket as she hurried across the slope to the two men. She spoke quietly, beyond earshot, taking a good spell to explain things to them. Fargo lay back and waited, and finally she returned and sank down beside him.

"I told them so now they're prepared for whatever I decide in the morning. They're pretty exhausted. They'll be turning in right away," Elise said.

"And you?" he asked.

"I'm tired, but I'm also on edge," she said, lying down beside him. "And you've learned when I'm on edge I need to relax."

"I kind of remember that," he said, and she stretched out beside him, turned, and lay half across his chest. Her fingers slowly opened the buttons that ran down the front of her dress until the top fell open. He looked at the long lovely curve of the shallow breasts as she pulled open the other buttons, shook her shoulders, and the top of the dress fell to her waist. He gave her a half-smile. "Figuring to change my mind?" he asked.

"I know better than that," Elise murmured.

"Good," Fargo said.

"I want more of you to remember, if that's what has to be," she said, pushed the rest of her dress down, and lay naked half across him, her slender body enticingly lovely, the long breasts moving together as she brought herself higher up on him. He opened his lips to welcome the soft breasts as she pressed them into his face. She rubbed their smoothness over his face and teased with each dark-red tip. He felt himself responding, growing quickly firm and hot. Elise kept her arms around him as she swung onto her back, pulling him atop her.

"Let me get these clothes off," Fargo said as she held him tightly over her.

"Let me," she whispered as she started to unbutton his shirt. As she did so, her long legs came up to clasp around his hips, and he felt the warmth of her even through his clothes. He was helping pull his shirt off, feeling the wonderfully soft touch of her breasts against his bare chest, when he heard the sound from behind. He half turned, just in time to see the upraised shovel over his head, and then it smashed down on him. Bright lights exploded through his head, scores of them, and then with the same suddenness, they snapped off and the world swam away and went black.

He didn't feel himself being lifted and carried. He didn't feel his gun being taken, and he didn't feel anything when he was thrown down the mine shaft. He didn't feel it when he hit the wooden floor of the first platform inside the mine, but, in the strange ways of the unconscious mind, he felt the sharpness of pain as he lay facedown inside the mine. It was as if the second sharp blow to his head had somehow shocked him into half consciousness. He lay still, but the total darkness had lifted and become a fuzzy grayness when he felt himself move one arm. He shook his head, and the grayness lightened further. The pain was not only in his head now, but in his shoulders and back. A half-consciousness was just beginning to form in his mind when the explosion erupted.

He heard it only as a dim, dull sound, a noise as if from a faraway place, but he was conscious of a number of smaller sounds that followed, and he was aware enough to feel the platform shake where he lay. Another sound came to him, sharper, a cracking sound, and he was aware he was falling. Then the blackness swept over him again, and there was nothing.

9

He had no idea how long it was until the blackness lifted again and feeling returned to his body, awareness fighting through his mind. But consciousness returned, slowly, and with it the pain in his head. He lay still, letting the mind reassert itself in its own time, not that he had a choice. Finally, he felt his eyes open and in his nostrils, the sharp acrid odor of dust. He blinked and saw nothing but blackness. He blinked again, but the blackness stayed, and he sat up. It took a moment for him to realize this blackness came not from inside but outside. The taste and odor of dust grew stronger in his nostrils and, wincing, he turned, half crawled, and felt rocks of various sizes under his hands.

He sat still and made his thoughts arrange themselves in an orderly fashion. Elise came back to him first, her breasts against his face, her legs wrapped around him, holding him in place atop her. The shovel materialized in his mind next, slamming down on his head. Then there was only the blackness until he had half wakened. He remembered the other sounds then, the explosion and the sounds that followed. He could put it all together now, everything falling into place. Elise swam into his thoughts. She hadn't gone to Chowder and Walters to tell them they might not go on come morning. She had gone to set her plans in motion. Then she had held his attention, held him physically.

Fargo uttered a silent curse as the events swirled through his mind. He'd been knocked unconscious and thrown into the mine shaft. He'd regained enough consciousness to hear the explosion. They had dynamited the mouth of the mine, and the other sounds he'd heard had been the rock and dirt falling in. He cursed again and began to crawl until he reached the one wall where the vertical ladder rose upward. He used his hands to feel his way as he climbed up the rungs until he suddenly had to stop. Huge pieces of rock blocked his way upward, so he left the ladder and climbed over more stones, some smaller ones dislodging to roll away while a trickle of dirt drifted down from above. He halted and felt with his hands as he peered over his head. But there was no light. The mine had been thoroughly sealed. He was trapped in blackness. He leaned against a piece of rock and knew all the things he'd do, all the efforts he'd have to make, and with bitterness spiraling through him, he knew they'd all be in vain.

But the human spirit demands effort, lives on hope, and all too soon it would live on desperation. That was the cycle, and he knew he would follow it. Perhaps most of all because he had no choice to do anything else. The total blackness told him two bitter truths. The mine was sealed by rock and dirt, sealed from even a glimmer of light or a trickle or air, and he was already aware of the preciousness of the air still in the shaft. He would use it up all too quickly, he knew, and the irony of his plight stabbed at him. He had to try to dig a way out, even if it seemed hopeless. He had to use his only tools, his hands and arms and feet, to try and dig himself free of his prison. But the harder he dug the more breath he'd use, and the more breath he used the quicker he'd deplete what little air there was in the mine.

But there was no alternative, except to sit and wait, but that was really not an alternative. The air would eventually evaporate by itself. His very act of breathing would use it up. Doing nothing would only prolong the inevitable. Again, he had only one choice, and he pushed himself onto his hands and knees and began to feel along the rocks above his head. When he found one that moved at the touch, he used his hands to pull at it until it came loose. A small funnel of dirt came down following the rock and struck him in the face. Wiping the dirt away, he began to dig at the dirt, using his fingers to pull and scrape and claw until he finally had to stop as his hands cramped.

He rested, let his fingers uncramp, and returned to the task, clawing and digging until he finally had to stop again. He sat back and used his foot to explore the dirt he had dug loose, and he felt dark disappointment sweep through him. There was so little, so pitifully little, he groaned. Resting until the pain in his fingers finally subsided enough for him to continue, he resumed the task. He clawed and dug, rested, and then returned, scraping and pulling, and from time to time he managed to pull away a rock. Each time it seemed a major victory, and the exhilaration prodded him to go on with renewed strength.

It became the pattern for his existence, clawing at the earth, digging and scraping with his fingers, resting, then clawing again until his hands, wrists, and arms grew so stiff he had to quit and stretch out. Hours became just a meaningless passage of time. The world was simply a black void in which he dug at the earth as though he were a mole or an earthworm. In between, he closed his eyes and took time to sleep only to wake with a start and return to work. But time did not stand still, though it seemed as though it did. He could measure its passing by its own set of painful, grim markers, the dryness that parched his throat, the increasing weakness of his entire body, and one more sign, the deadliest of all. Each breath was growing more difficult as the air grew thinner. His chest felt more and more painful as he scraped and dug and clawed in his stygian void.

He finally lost all sense of time and became aware that his efforts were growing more halting, his need to stop and rest more frequent. The burning inside his chest grew stronger, and he felt his chest heaving with every breath. He guessed that with the snatches of sleep he'd had to take at least a day had passed, perhaps two, but he knew it was only a guess conjured out of pain and blackness and the suspension of time. Finally, his fingers raw and sore, his body trembling with weakness, and his chest afire, he sank against one wall and let the specter of final defeat sweep through him.

The only sound was the rasping of his breath, and he lay still, painfully aware that for all his digging and pain, he had made little progress. The stones, dirt, and rock of the collapsed shaft seemed hardly touched. They hovered over his head with a silent, stygian glower. He lay not in a collapsed mine, he realized, but in a tomb, his tomb, and he cursed softly as he felt the weakness taking over his body. Moving even a hand had become a terrible effort, and he tried to sit up as straight as he could in order to gulp in the few draughts of what little air remained.

Bitter, silent curses were all he had left to rage against the inexorable hand of fate. He felt the air vanishing, not even the slightest movement of it against his face. The terrible realization lay upon him. He was simply waiting for the suffocation that would come when the last bit of air vanished from the mine.

The moment was not far away, he knew, and the helplessness was a cloak around his shoulders when he heard a sound, a faint, pinging noise. He frowned, blinked in the utter blackness, and strained his ears. The sound came again, a faint hammering, from directly above. He used the last ounce of his strength to push away from the wall, rested on hands and knees, and stared up at the ceiling of stone and dirt. The hammering continued, steady, still distant, but steady. Fargo opened his mouth to call out and found he could muster only a hoarse croak out of his parched throat.

He felt dizziness sweep over him as he stared up through the blackness, and he lowered his head as his breath wheezed through his chest. But suddenly he felt something against his cheek, a soft, delicate touch. It took him a moment before he realized what he felt, and his lips formed the word: *air*. He gasped, drew in a breath, and felt the small but steady stream of air touch his face again. It was filtering down from directly above him and meant but one thing. Rocks had been dislodged, an opening created that let air instantly rush downward. Despair was suddenly flung aside as hope spiraled through him. He could breathe properly, and he pulled the new stream of air into his throat and lungs. Suddenly, the total blackness shattered away, and a ray of light streamed into the shaft almost directly over his head. A rock had been broken, the crude window opened into the blackness. "Jesus," Fargo breathed. "Thank God."

He lifted his head and saw the jagged opening, the bright light of day appearing behind a head looking down. "You down there?" a voice said, and Fargo nodded as he found his own voice on the wings of the air he could now pull into his throat.

"Yes, Jesus, yes," he said. The head, half silhouetted with the brightness of the day behind it, moved and took form, dark blond hair, and he caught the flick of a ponytail. "Toby," he said, swallowing hard. "Toby."

"Wait," she said, and he saw her head draw back, caught the swing of a pickaxe, and then the sound of it as Toby hammered the edges of the hole to enlarge it. The hammering dislodged more rocks, and he dodged one that fell in at him. But the hole opened wide enough for him to fit through, and Toby disappeared for a moment to return with a length of lariat. She lowered it, and he tied it around his waist. "I've the other end wrapped around my saddle horn," she called down. "Ready?"

"Ready," he said and swung his feet up against the walls of the shaft and braced himself as the rope began to pull him up out of the mine shaft. His shoulders brushed the edge of the rock as he reached the top, and he fell out onto the ground. Toby called the horse to a halt and ran back to where he lay drawing in deep draughts of air. She helped him take the lariat from around his waist, and finally he pushed up onto one elbow to peer at her.

"You're sure a sight for sore eyes," he said. "What the hell brought you back here?"

"I met Elise, Rick Chowder, and Ernie. They were on

their way back to her place. I'd just finished a patch of wild cherries I'd had for breakfast. They were passing on a road below me," Toby said. "I asked where you were. Elise told me she'd paid you, and you rode off north. They went on, then."

"Why didn't you believe them?" Fargo asked.

"I did at first, then I got to thinking it didn't sound right," Toby said.

"Why not?"

"You said you were going to come visit me," Toby reminded him. "You're not the kind to say something and not do it. I knew something was wrong. I felt it," she said.

"So you rode back."

"That's right. When I saw the mouth of the mine caved in, I knew they'd dynamited it, and I knew you had to be inside. What I didn't know was whether you were alive or not, so I took a pickaxe and started digging."

"Thank God," Fargo said and pulled himself to his feet. "Guess I know now what happened on that cliff," he said and folded his arms around her. "I owe you, Toby, big time." She didn't answer, but she didn't pull away. He finally stepped away. He glanced across to where the Ovaro stood and saw at once that the big Henry was gone from its saddle case. Automatically, his hand went to the holster on his hip and he cursed as he felt only empty air. "They didn't need a saddle, but a good Henry and a fine Colt will fetch a fancy price," he muttered. "How long was I down there?" he asked Toby.

"The first night and I've been digging for two days," Toby said.

"Enough time for them to be back at her place," Fargo said. "Let's go."

"It's a hard ride. You up to it?" Toby questioned.

"We'll take it slow," he said and pulled himself onto the Ovaro as Toby gathered her things and swung in beside him. He led the way down the slope, retracing the route he'd blazed until night fell. He found a small pond bordered by wild corn, and Toby made a small fire to boil the corn. Later, she settled onto his bedroll with him, and it took only moments for her high, round breasts to press against his naked chest, the barrel-ribbed figure rubbing its compact firmness against him. Her lips pressed his, a soft, sweet taste, and he held her to him. "I hurt you. I'm sorry for that," he said.

"You had no way to be sure. I guess I knew that. I just hated not being believed," she said. "But it's all past now, forgotten."

"Prove it," he teased.

"Love to," she said, and he felt her hand reach down, her fingers curling around him. She gave a little gasp as she found he was already responding to her, hot and throbbing to her touch. She tightened her fingers, caressed, quickened her motion, and she quickly came over him, pressing her warm, convex little belly into his groin and crying out at the warm soft-hard touch of his maleness. She slid downward, then up, and her wet warmth came over him, an encompassing, wonderful embrace. She proceeded to prove she had forgiven him until, with a throaty scream, she cried out in ecstasy, a final affirmation wrapped in delight. Later, when she lay against him, still making little noises of sweet satisfaction, he lifted himself onto one elbow and enjoyed the curvy roundness of her.

"You're still convinced there's a map?" he asked.

"Yes," Toby said.

"And you're still going to look for it," he said.

"Yes," she said. "You don't think I should."

"With all that's happened, I'm wondering if the whole thing might be better left alone. Some things are just jinxed. Nothing good ever comes out of them," Fargo said.

She shrugged. "If I can find it, it could be my way out of here," Toby said. "And a comfortable life." She pulled him half over her. "Stay a little longer. Give me a little more time to look before you go."

He nodded. He owed her at least that. She snuggled herself against him, and he slept with her until the new day came to wake them both. She rode beside him as he retraced steps, Pagoda Peak at their back now, and reached the long fields of the dwarf sunflowers, then the dangerous, narrow passage where the north wind blew in their faces this time. Night came, and once again Toby made the little glen Fargo found ring with her cries of delight until, satiated, she slept in his arms. They made good time when morning came, and it was midday when they neared the rolling hills and the drop in the land that meant they were closing in on the Farrell house.

"I'm going on alone. I don't want to be worrying about you," he said. "You make a wide circle and go to your place."

"What are you going to do when you get there?" she asked.

"Don't know. It'll depend on her," Fargo said. "You have a sheriff in Hobsonville?"

"Old Harry Watrell," Toby said. "He's not much of a sheriff, but if you bring her in, I guess he can arrest her."

"I'll do that much. She tried to kill me," Fargo said.

"You're just giving her another chance. She's got her gun, yours, and her two hands. You don't have anything," Toby said and drew a Remington revolver from the waistband of her skirt. "Take this," she said and handed him the weapon. He held it for a moment, took in the six-shot, single-action pistol, a serviceable gun, but not nearly as accurate as his Colt. But accuracy wouldn't be that important, he knew, and dropped the gun into his empty holster. She leaned over and kissed him. "Be careful," she said and sent her horse into a trot, not looking back. He moved the Ovaro forward when she rode from sight and threaded his way through the maples until he came in sight of the stone-based Farrell house.

He halted, scanned the barn near the house, then surveyed the house. Nothing moved, so he dismounted to creep forward on foot, circling to come closer from behind the barn. The barn door hung open, and he glanced in. The buckboard with the yellow wheels was missing, the barn empty, no horses inside, either. A frown touched his brow as he moved forward, one hand on the Remington at his hip. He went to the side window of the house, peered in, and saw no one. He waited, let minutes go by, and still saw no one. Finally, he crept to the front of the house, where the door swung open at his touch. Gun in hand, he went in, listened, and heard nothing. He moved through the front rooms into Elise's bedroom, and his frown deepened.

The closet door hung open, the clothes gone from inside it, along with any traveling bags that should have been there. He whirled and stalked from the house, his lips drawn back. She'd returned to get her things and run. Holstering the Remington, his eyes scanned the ground. He quickly picked up the tracks of the buckboard and two horses. She'd left with company, Chowder and Ernie Walters. He called the Ovaro, swung onto the horse, and followed the tracks westward. He paused after he'd gone a few thousand yards, dismounted, and felt the marks of the wagon wheels, then the hoofprints. They hadn't been gone long, he took note, the tracks still soft and firm at the edges. Not more than a few hours, he guessed, and he returned to the saddle and put the pinto into a fast canter. He'd ridden almost two hours when he slowed. They had stayed due west on low paths easy for the buckboard to take, and he followed the trail up a narrow path bordered on both sides by forests of hackberry.

Elise had elected to go around Hobsonville, avoiding the town, and he reined up at a place where the path crossed another. He frowned down at the marks of three more horses where the tracks met. They had halted, he saw, and the three horses had gone their way south while the buckboard, Chowder, and Walters continued north. Again, Fargo followed and cast a glance skyward where he saw the sun touching the tops of the distant mountains. The trail wound through a flat stretch of land dotted with thickets of heavy brush and clumps of relatively short hawthorns. The land dipped suddenly, and Fargo saw the buckboard, Elise at the reins, the two men riding alongside her.

He turned the Ovaro onto higher ground into a line of hawthorns and hurried the horse forward until he was opposite the travelers but still in the trees. Fargo cursed silently. There was no spot for an ambush, no way he could cover all three of them at once. He thought of following until night fell, but discarded the thought. Darkness would be a double-edged sword. It could help him get closer, but it could also help them use the dark as cover. If he attacked by night and didn't get everyone at once, which appeared less and less likely, his element of surprise would be gone. He swore again and spurred the Ovaro forward to where he saw a formation of rocks that rose up at the edge of the path. They'd pass below it, the buckboard just skirting the edge of the rocks.

Reaching the gray granite formation, he spotted a low, flat ledge, dismounted, and left the horse behind the taller rocks as he crawled forward onto the flat ledge. Waiting on his stomach, he saw the buckboard appear, roll toward him, and he saw that Chowder and Walters had fallen in behind the buckboard to ride single file. It would offer his best chance, he realized, and his eyes focused on Elise as she drove the rig directly below where he lay. Her traveling bags were inside the rear of the buckboard. A rifle rested against the back of the wagon seat, but it was a Winchester army issue. His Henry and his Colt were not to be seen. The buckboard passed where he lay, then Rick Chowder followed, and last, some six feet back, Ernie Walters.

Fargo tensed his body and waited till Ernie Walters was directly beneath him. Raising himself up, he dived from the ledge. He landed atop Walters, taking the man out of the saddle with him as Walters gave a half-shout, half-grunt of surprise. He hit the ground, one arm wrapped around the man's neck, wrestled him back to the side of the road, and pressed Toby's Remington into his temple. Rick Chowder had pulled to a halt and had already leaped to the ground before Elise rolled the wagon to a stop. Fargo saw her climb into the rear of the buckboard and scoop up the rifle, bring it to her shoulder.

"Surprise," Fargo rasped and saw Elise's eyes open wide.

"Jesus," she breathed. But she kept the rifle to her shoulder. Chowder, six-gun in hand, also stared at Fargo in surprise.

"Let him go," Chowder called.

"Drop your guns," Fargo said, holding Walters in front of him as a shield, the Remington pressed to the man's temple. He saw Rick Chowder cast a quick glance at Elise, uncertainty in his eyes, but she didn't look back at him. "I get nervous, I press too hard or my finger jerks and he's dead," Fargo said. "Sure thing." He saw Rick Chowder swallow hard and cast another glance at Elise, fear and pleading in it this time. Elise felt the glance, Fargo knew, but again she paid no heed to it.

"Drop the guns," Ernie Walters cried out. "Jesus, do what he says."

"Listen to the man," Fargo said. "You don't want to make me kill him, do you?"

"No, don't do that," Ernie Walters pleaded.

"Take it easy," Rick Chowder called out.

"Shut up," Elise hissed and kept the rifle at her shoulder.

"You're not good enough shots to get me without killing him," Fargo said.

"He's right," Chowder said.

"Yes, he is," Elise said. Fargo's eyes were on her, and he felt surprise erupt through him, his mouth falling open

141

as he started to protest. He saw Elise's finger tighten on the trigger of the rifle, and the next thing he knew was Ernie Walters's head exploding into a cascade of blood and bone.

"Goddamn" he swore as he flung himself backward into the trees. Another rifle shot grazed his shoulder, and still another whistled past his head as he fell. Elise was firing seriously, and then he heard Rick Chowder join in. But Fargo was on his stomach in the trees, and he spun himself around, firing the Remington as he did. But Elise had leaped from the buckboard to hide behind it in a crouch, and Rick Chowder had flattened himself against the rocks as he fired. Fargo lifted his head enough to catch a glimpse of Elise as she rolled from the buckboard into the trees, and he breathed a string of curses.

He hadn't expected her move. He had misjudged her total amorality. His mistake, he realized, recalling how she had coldly entombed him. There was no chance to bring them in, now, no chance to end it without more killing. Perhaps there never had been, he reflected. He saw movement in the trees on his side of the road and raised the Remington as the leaves moved again. He fired, saw the shot snap off a low branch, but the figure behind drop low, and he flicked the chamber open on the revolver and cursed. There was only one bullet left in the gun. A movement across the road caught his eye, and he saw Rick Chowder dart from the rocks to run behind the horse at the buckboard. The man darted again around the horse and dived into the trees where Elise hid. Listening, Fargo heard Rick Chowder crawl forward and halt.

"You shouldn't have done that," he heard Rick Chowder call out. "You shouldn't have killed Ernie."

"Shut up," Elise's voice came back. "I had to do it."

"No, no you didn't. That was rotten," Chowder returned.

"You're next," Fargo shouted, cutting in to their exchange. "She doesn't give a shit about you."

"Shut up, you bastard," Elise half screamed and then, her voice lowering, called to Chowder. "See what you've done, you fool? He thinks he can get to us. Shut up and back me up."

Fargo heard no reply from Rick Chowder, but he caught the movement of the trees again. Elise was crawling forward, closer. But she had grown smarter. She inched forward, halted, then pushed herself sideways and crawled forward again at a different spot, not giving him a chance to draw a bead on her movements. But some six feet behind, the leaves also moved as Chowder followed her. Fargo raised the Remington. Chowder was angered at Elise, but he'd back her up. He'd no choice. He was a partner in crime. Fargo's eyes narrowed, sighted along the barrel of the revolver, and as Rick Chowder crawled forward again, he fired just back of the first leaves that moved.

"Ow, Jesus," Chowder's voice cried out. "My arm, he got my arm." Fargo waited and finally Elise answered, no concern in her voice, only a rush of excitement.

"He fired only one shot. He would've fired another if he could. He's out of bullets," she said, her voice rising, and Fargo cursed her instant cunning. He half rose and dived from the trees to where Ernie Walters's shattered body lay sprawled. He was reaching for the gun in the man's holster when the shots rang out, one slamming a fraction of an inch from his face, another hurtling into the man's gun. Fargo saw the chamber of the pistol split as the bullet plowed into it, and he kicked his heels into the ground and spun himself back into the trees. "Let's get him," Elise screamed, and Fargo heard her running forward. He began to run in a crouch, not caring about stealth, setting a zigzag pattern through the trees. He ran directly at Elise for a moment, broke away, ran to the right, then circled.

He glimpsed her figure moving after him, halting, trying to center him in her sights. Rick Chowder appeared, moving slowly after her, whirling in fright as Fargo darted behind him, then to his left, then his right. Suddenly, Fargo stopped running and dropped to the ground. He was silent as a rattler waiting to strike. He lay flat, but he could see Rick Chowder stopped only a few feet in front of him, holding his right arm to his chest, the revolver in his left hand. Elise was partly hidden a dozen feet farther. The man started to move toward him again. "No, stupid, don't move," Elise spit out. "Wait. Listen."

Fargo allowed a tight smile to touch his lips. The man was no hunter. He didn't know how to wait. He hadn't the discipline of experience or of instinct, and he had an arm that burned with pain. He wouldn't hold out long. Elise was another matter. She hadn't real discipline, either, but she had the cunning self-preservation of a fox. She'd remain the real problem. He lay motionless, hardly breathing, and let the seconds tick off, knowing they would seem minutes to Rick Chowder. Almost on cue, the man raised his voice. "The hell with this. I'm going to find him," Chowder snarled and started forward.

"No, be quiet," Elise snapped.

144

"Screw you. I want to get to a doc," the man fired back. Fargo grunted softly and let the noise of Chowder's pushing through the brush cover the faint sound of his hand drawing the double-edged throwing knife from its calf holster. The thin blade in his palm, Fargo saw the man come closer, a half-dozen feet to his right. He took aim, raised his arm, and with a quick, powerful motion sent the blade hurtling through the foliage. It hit his target, Chowder's wounded arm, sinking to the hilt in the man's forearm. "Ow, God," Chowder screamed in pain, spun, and fired, emptying his gun as Fargo stayed crouched till he finished and then hurtled forward. The man tried to bring his empty gun down in a slashing arc with his left hand, but Fargo easily parried the blow and shot back a left hook that caught Chowder flush on the jaw.

A shot rang out just as Rick Chowder flew backward. Fargo saw his body shudder as the bullet thudded into him, seem to hang in midair for a brief moment, and then collapse to the ground. Fargo was diving to one side as two more shots rang out, both grazing his shoulder blades. He hit the ground, rolled, and came up behind a tree trunk. Another shot slammed into the base of the tree, and then he heard the sharp click of an empty chamber followed by Elise's curse. The next sound was Elise running through the brush, breaking off young branches as she raced away. He rose and listened for a moment. She was running back to the buckboard. He dug his feet into the soft earth of the forest and gave chase, crashing through the brush in a straight line as he followed the sound of her path.

He reached the road seconds after she had raced into the open and saw her half turn to glance back at him as she came alongside the buckboard. The rifle still in her hands, she pulled herself onto the wagon, took hold of the rifle by the stock, and waited for him to reach her side. "Give it up," Fargo called to her and started to climb onto the wagon when she tried to smash the rifle stock into his face. He dropped back, ducked away from the blow, and had to twist aside again as she swung the rifle in a half-arc at him. Ducking under the blow, he tried climbing up at her again, but she was quick, and her backhanded swing grazed his temple. This time he stopped trying to climb onto the wagon. Instead, he stayed low as he lunged forward. He was prepared for the rifle stock that smashed into his back between his shoulder blades. He had his muscles tightened, but still winced at the force of the blow as he got his hands around her ankles and pulled.

Elise went backward off balance, hit hard against the seat of the buckboard, and uttered a half-cry half-curse of pain. He yanked her forward, knocked the rifle out of her hands, and pulled her with him out of the buckboard. She hit the ground on her back and gasped in pain again, and he dragged her away from the buckboard wheel as the horse reared and the wagon rolled forward. "Whoa, easy, now," he said, grabbing hold of the horse's cheek strap, and the animal quickly calmed down. Elise was pushing to her feet, grimacing in pain, as Fargo faced her, but he saw only sullen anger in her eyes. "Why?" he asked. "It wasn't just saving the money you owed me."

She sniffed, and he saw the disdain come into her eyes. "That was part of it," she said.

"Give me the other part."

"Nobody walks out on me," she said. "I say when it's over. I say when you leave and when you stay."

"Not with me. Not with anybody anymore," Fargo said.

Scorn came into her eyes. "You going to hang around until they bring in a judge and give me a trial? That'll take a long while."

"No, but I'll come back," he said and saw her eyes grow narrow. "I'll make a special point of it. You're worth it, honey. Doesn't that make you feel good?"

"Go to hell," she muttered. He laughed, whistled, and waited as he heard the Ovaro make its way down from the rocks.

"Where's my Henry and my Colt?" he asked Elise.

"Sold them," she said, and he remembered where she had met with someone. "Fetched a very nice price, they did."

He reached into the buckboard and pulled her purse out before she could catch hold of it. The money lay open inside the purse, and he took it out and pushed it into his pocket. "This'll help me buy a new set," he said. "Now get on the driver's seat. I'll be riding right behind you all the way back to Hobsonville." He watched as Elise climbed onto the buckboard and turned it around before he swung in behind her. He stayed back a dozen or so feet as she drove the wagon down the path and across a flat meadow. Dusk began to fall over the land, and he realized night would descend before they reached Hobsonville. He wasn't happy at the thought, but there was no place he could run, and he stayed behind the wagon as dusk turned into dark.

A half-moon rose, and the roadway curved, becoming uneven and lined with young maples. She made no effort to talk to him, and the road took a dip downward when she pulled to a halt. She called back without turning her head. "He's gone lame," she said. Fargo brought the pinto closer to the rear of the wagon, slid to the ground, and walked to the horse hitched to the rig. "Front left foreleg, I'd guess," Elise said. Fargo halted at the horse, squatted down, and ran his hand carefully along the horse's cannon bone, down the tendon, checked the fetlock, and was about to lift the hoof to examine the pastern when he heard the sharp snap of the reins. Elise's command followed, and the horses bolted forward. He felt the end of the left wagon shaft slam into his shoulder and the horse's forequarters hit against him. He went sprawling, but instinct made him draw his legs up, and his instant reaction time kept him from being run over by the two left wheels of the wagon.

He lay on his side for a moment, legs drawn up, aware that only split seconds had stood between him and broken or badly bruised legs. He straightened out, leaped to his feet, and swung onto the pinto. Elise was racing the buckboard full speed down the roadway, careening around curves, and he saw the rig take one curve on two wheels as he sent the Ovaro after her. He was gaining on her when he saw her take another sharp curve at full speed. He was watching as the buckboard's left rear wheel hit hard against a rock at the edge of the curve. The wagon skittered on two wheels, the rear going up in the air, and he saw Elise's form pitched headfirst out of the wagon.

His lips drew back as he saw her hurtle into a tree, and he winced as he heard the sharp, cracking sound. He reined to a halt and leaped from the saddle. When he reached the tree, he saw her face smashed against the bark, her head driven halfway down into her body at a grotesque angle so that her head and neck seemed no higher than her shoulders. He stared down and saw that Elise Farrell had drawn her last breath. He turned away and let a deep sigh escape him. Pulling himself onto the Ovaro, he moved forward past the buckboard, which had halted a few dozen yards down the road. *I decide when it's over,* she had said. She had done precisely that, he thought as he rode on.

10

When Fargo reached Toby's place, a small oasis of light spread from the house. She had every lamp in the place lighted, and when she came to the door, she held a kerosene lamp in one hand. Fargo swung from the saddle and let the horse go free. He'd paused in Hobsonville to give the sheriff directions to the "terrible accident" west of town. Now he read the questions in Toby's eyes. "It's finished," he said and told her everything that had happened. She studied his face when he finished.

"You'd like to feel sorry for her," she said, and he allowed a half-shrug. "But you can't," Toby added, and his shoulders shrugged again. "You shouldn't. She tried to kill you," Toby added.

"Twice," he grunted and focused on Toby. "Looks like you've spent the time searching," he said.

"Yes. Didn't find anything. I was about to go to the barn when you rode up," she said.

"The barn?"

"Amos often worked there. Stu Farrell spent a lot of time there with him," Toby said.

"Let's go," Fargo said and fell in step with Toby as she strode to the barn. Inside, he again took in the rotted wood at the joists of the ceiling, the eaten-away bottom edges of the walls, and the cracked and splintered boards. "This place is ready to fall down," he commented. She set the lamp on the floor, closed the barn door to keep the light concentrated inside, and her eyes went to the cross timbers of the roof. He saw numerous holes in the timbers with some portions rotted away. "You thinking up there?" he questioned.

"There are plenty of places," Toby said. "There's a ladder in the corner."

"I'll get it," he said and moved across the floor, picking his way past pieces of a plow, rakes, assorted shovels, and one long-handled three-pronged pitchfork. He reached the tall ladder and carried it back to Toby, then set it down securely with the top rungs touching the nearest roof beam. "This whole damn place is rickety," he said.

"I'll go up. I'm lightest," she said and started to climb the ladder. She had gone only a few rungs when a curse burst from Fargo's lips.

"Christ, stop," he said as his nostrils filled with the dark, pungent, sweet-sour odor, and Toby halted and drew a deep breath.

"The grizzly," she gasped.

"I didn't smell him. He must've been downwind of us. Goddamn, he's right outside," Fargo hissed.

As if in reply, the deep, savage growl rumbled through the air, and two huge paws pushed against the barn wall. Fargo saw the old, cracked wood bend. Toby jumped down from the ladder as the bear stood up on his hind legs and pushed again at the wall. Again, the boards bent, and another chilling growl rent the air. Fargo felt Toby close beside him. "We don't have a damn slingshot," he muttered and listened to the grizzly's shuffling steps suddenly turn into a thudding sound as over a thousand pounds of massive bulk began to run. "Shit," Fargo spit out as the giant grizzly crashed into the barn, going full speed.

The rotten and splintered wood gave way, and the huge grizzled brown form crashed into the barn. Fargo yanked Toby back with him as the nearest roof timber hurtled down and smashed onto the floor as the remainder of the barn shuddered and smaller bits of woods fell. Fargo saw the grizzly on the other side of the fallen timber, the small eyes glittering as the tremendous body started to step over the timber to come at them. Suddenly Toby's voice exploded beside him. "Look," she said, and Fargo glanced down to see the piece of paper that had fallen out of the roof beam. It lay faceup, the lines and marks on it unmistakably only one thing. "The map," Toby screamed. "The goddamn map." Bursting from his side, she rushed for the map.

"No," he shouted as the grizzly swerved and went for her. The giant bear reached the map at the same moment Toby did, uttered a growl of fury as it lunged at her. Toby tried to duck away from the huge, furred body and reach down to scoop up the map, but with the quickness people always underestimated, one huge paw slammed into her. It was a glancing blow, yet it knocked her a dozen feet. "Stay away from him," Fargo yelled as he saw Toby roll and get to her feet. But Toby ran forward again as the grizzly half rose on his hind legs and pawed the air. She circled, stayed low, again tried to reach the map where it lay on the floor. The bear roared a snarl and came at her with his swinging motion that was so deceptive. Toby again tried to reach the map, but this time she was quick enough to duck the swipe of a giant paw. "Get

152

away," Fargo called again as he ran forward, circled to the rear of the bear, and kicked with all his strength at the thick, furred rump.

If he felt the blow, the grizzly gave no sign as he lunged at Toby again. As he came forward, his left hind foot hit the kerosene lamp. The lamp shattered at once as it fell over and tongues of kerosene-fed flame instantly licked across the dry wood of the floor. Fargo saw the flame catch onto the map and heard Toby's scream. "No," she shouted and ran forward with heedless desperation, half screaming and half sobbing. She tried to scoop the burning map up from almost under the grizzly's legs, but the bear did the scooping, sweeping Toby up in his paws. He held her up, massive head only inches from her, jaws open, lips pulled back to show his tremendous yellow fangs.

Fargo, cursing Toby as well as the bear, took hold of the only implement even resembling a weapon, the three-pronged pitchfork on the floor. As the bear held Toby for a moment longer in the air as though she were a rag doll, Fargo leaped forward, knowing that from where he was, he had only one spot that could hurt the massive form of bone, muscle, and sinew. He plunged the pitchfork into the bear's right hind foot and felt the prongs go through flesh and into the floor. With a tremendous roar the grizzly dropped Toby as he whirled. Fargo yanked the pitchfork free and twisted away from the swipe of a wide forepaw that brushed the hair back on his head. He glimpsed Toby on the floor, half-conscious, only a few feet from the map that was burning itself into ashes.

The grizzly was coming at him, roaring, great fangs bared, and Fargo gave ground as he clutched the pitchfork. The facts that he knew all too well leaped up at him again. He faced a creature of massive power protected by dense fur, tremendous muscle, heavy bones with a huge, thick skull, a creature that could be stopped by only the heaviest rifle shell, and then only if struck in the exact right place. Backing as the giant form came at him, Fargo knew he had but one ridiculously slim chance. He had to reach the bear's brain with the pitchfork. It was the one vital avenue left to him. But he also knew he hadn't the strength to plunge the prongs deeply enough. No man had. He had to let the grizzly's thousand-plus pounds do the work for him.

The bear increased speed as it came for him. Fargo took another two steps backward and let himself fall on his back on the floor. The grizzly came at once, reared up, and then dropped his huge form downward, jaws open to rip into his prey. Fargo forced himself to wait another split second and then brought the pitchfork up. He felt his arms shudder as the grizzly drove downward with all his weight and impaled himself on the three prongs. Fargo felt the thick, coarse fur brush against his face for an instant, but the bear pulled back and rose on his hind legs, a terrible cry of roaring fury and pain coming from him. Standing upright, almost ten feet tall, the bear pawed at the long-handled pole that stuck into his head. The two end prongs had been driven deep through his eyes and the middle prong into the big snout.

Using his paws, the bear pulled the pitchfork out of his head, and, still roaring in a combination of pure pain and pure rage, he moved backward out of the barn. He lumbered in a half-circle, first one way, then the other as he pawed at his face. He kept the half-turns as his head lowered closer to the ground, and he continued to make erratic movements as Fargo pushed to his feet and followed outside. He watched the huge, dark form stumble, get up, stumble again, and then go down on his front legs. He stayed that way, tried to rise, almost did, and fell forward again, but this time the rest of the massive form fell forward. Fargo stepped closer, saw the bear's thick legs kick out, first the front ones, then the rear, and finally stiffen and grow still.

Hearing the deep breath of air that came from him, Fargo turned and went into the shattered barn. Toby had come around, and she was on her knees before the ashes of the map as the still burning kerosene licked at nearby pieces of wood. The mist blue eyes were mistier than usual as they looked up at him. "I told you there was a map," she murmured, her voice catching.

"So you did." He nodded. "And you damn near got yourself killed over it." She said nothing, and he lifted her to her feet and walked out of the barn with her. They made a wide circle around the dark brown, massive form as they went to the house and closed the door. "What now?" he asked her.

"I want to leave here," Toby said. "Not in the morning. Now. There's nothing to keep me here. I'll get my things together, and we can leave."

"Suit yourself," Fargo said and watched Toby begin to put things into traveling sacks.

"I've friends in Kansas. I'll go visit with them before I decide what I'll be doing next. Can you get me to a stage for Kansas?" Toby asked.

"I'll do better. I'll take you. I've people to see down that way," Fargo said. "I'll get your horse saddled while you finish." He left her, called the quarterhorse, coaxed and soothed by voice, and finally the horse carefully returned to be saddled. Finished when Toby emerged with her bags, he loaded everything onto the horse and climbed onto the Ovaro. "What happens to this place?" he asked as they rode away.

"Somebody will take it over. I don't care. It was a home while I was here with Amos. Now it's just a house. I'll keep the good memories and take time to forget the bad," she said. Fargo led the way east and south, found a glen near a pond when the moon reached the midnight sky, and set out his bedroll. Toby came to lay beside him, her soft, warm skin welcome, a reminder that the world held pleasure as well as pain. "Just hold me, Fargo," she murmured, and he did just that as she fell asleep and the night grew late. Finally, when the morning sky returned, he woke, washed, and dressed, and was sitting on a log, staring across the morning mists when she came to sit beside him. She wore only a shirt that she held closed with one hand as she sank down on a bed of soft spineleaf moss. "What are you thinking about?" she asked.

"Gypsies," he said with a wry smile. "Gypsies and their tarot cards."

"What are they?"

"Tarot cards are special cards they have, very, very old cards. They read them and then tell your fortune," Fargo said.

"Sounds like a con job," she said dismissively.

"Exactly what I thought, only now I'm not so sure anymore," Fargo said, and she frowned at him. "They told me I was going to be killed, torn apart, ripped to little pieces. They were awfully close to being right."

"But they weren't," Toby said. "It didn't happen."

"They were too close. I know I won't be so quick to laugh off Gypsies and their tarot cards," he said.

Toby leaned closer, mist blue eyes searching his face.

"I'll tell your fortune," she said. "You're going to make love to me from here to Kansas, and that's a prediction you can count on coming true." Her blouse fell open as she pulled him down to the soft bed of moss, and before the morning was full, she proved the passion of prediction and the prediction of passion. He happily embraced both.

LOOKING FORWARD!
The following is the opening
section from the next novel in the exciting
Trailsman series from Signet:

THE TRAILSMAN # 177
COLORADO WOLF PACK

1861—Southwest Colorado Territory,
where the peaks touch the sky,
the women are willing,
and lead flies thick and fast . . .

Few things can get a man's attention faster than having the business end of a gun jammed into the base of his spine.

One moment Skye Fargo was strolling along a rutted dirt track that passed between two short rows of tents and cabins, the next a bulky form sprang out of the darkness and a pistol was shoved into the small of his back. Instantly, the big man froze.

"This is a warning, friend," declared a voice that reminded Fargo of gravel rattling down a slope. "If you know what's good for you, you'll quit asking questions about that old coot, McDermott. Savvy?"

Fargo knew better, but he could not help saying, "The last I heard, this is a free country, mister. I can do what I damn well please."

"You can if you want to die."

The back of Fargo's skull exploded in searing pain. His legs buckled and he sagged to his knees, struggling to stay conscious. No attempt was made to strip him of his Colt, but a hand did knock his hat off and roughly grab him by the hair. His head was snapped back. He caught a whiff of foul breath laced with liquor.

"This was your only warning, jackass," his attacker growled into his ear. "Keep on poking around and you'll be pushing up fireweed come spring."

A boot slammed into Fargo's kidney, adding to his agony. He slumped onto his elbows as footsteps rapidly sped into the night. The only other sounds were the nicker of a horse at a hitchrack, and tinny music from the ramshackle excuse for a saloon farther down the street.

Fargo did not stay bent over for long. Gritting his teeth against the torment, he straightened, reclaimed his white hat, and slowly stood. For a few seconds the world spun and wobbled as if it were a kid's top, then his piercing lake-blue eyes cleared. He slapped dust from his buckskins with his hat, placed it on his head, and headed for the saloon, his anger mounting with every stride.

The town, if such it could be called, wasn't on any map. It had sprung up within the past six months as miners, settlers, and others started flocking deep into the Rocky Mountains from points east.

Some folks called it Pfeifferville, others San Juan, still others Pagosa Springs in honor of the hot mineral springs nearby. It was located high in the Colorado Rockies. The San Juan Mountains surrounded it on three sides. To the northeast reared the Continental Divide.

It was as remote a place as a man was likely to find

anywhere. There was no marshal or sheriff or lawman of any kind, not even a justice of the peace. If someone were wronged, they had to take the matter into their own hands or turn the other cheek.

Fargo wasn't the forgiving sort. Pausing, he pulled his Colt, flipped open the loading gate, and made sure he had five beans in the wheel, as a Texan might say. He whirled the pistol back into his holster and walked on. Ahead, he noticed a patch of ground at the corner of the whiskey mill. Thanks to lantern light spilling through the only window, he saw something that brought a grim smile to his mouth.

The saloon did not have batwing doors. In fact, there wasn't a door of any kind. The owner, an Irishman named Sullivan, was too lazy to make one and too cheap to have one shipped in. He merely tacked a blanket over the opening every night before turning in and took it down the next day. Since everyone knew that he slept on the bar with a scattergun cradled in his arms, no one tried to help themselves to his stock.

On this particular night the saloon was crowded. Smoke hung heavy in the air. So did the odor of alcohol and sweat. Jumbled voices rose to the rafters.

Fargo stepped to the right with his back to the log wall as soon as he entered. His thumbs hooked in his gunbelt, he let his eyes adjust to the glare. No one paid much attention to him. Men were drinking, gambling, or joking with the two fallen doves who worked for Sullivan. He studied the feet of everyone in sight. Most wore boots. A few favored moccasins. Only two men in the whole establishment had on store-bought shoes.

When he did not find what he was looking for, Fargo sidled along the wall, passing a table where four men played five card stud. A grizzled character holding his cards close to his chest glanced up sharply, as if he suspected Fargo trying to peek at his hand.

"Hey, you there!" he said gruffly, his right cheek crammed with chewing tobacco, his face looked swollen. "I don't like anyone standin' behind me when I'm playin'."

Fargo had stopped to study the footwear of the men at the bar. A beefy character at the very end caught his interest. The man had just been given a whiskey and was raising the glass. He was going to go on but fingers plucked at his sleeve.

"I don't like bein' ignored, stranger," the card player snapped. An old Dragoon Army Model revolver was wedged under his wide brown belt, and he put a hand on the butt. "Give me one good reason why I shouldn't get up out of this chair and teach you some manners."

Some of the other men snickered.

Fargo looked the cantankerous cuss right in the eyes. "I can think of one."

"Oh? Let me hear it."

Lowering his hand near his Colt, Fargo said in a flat tone, "You can't finish the game if you're dead."

The man reddened and started to rise. He even began to draw the Dragoon. But the next moment he stopped. His brow wrinkled. He chewed on his lower lip a few seconds while staring at Fargo's gun hand. When he looked back up at Fargo's face, he swallowed hard and said softly, "You have a good point. So let's not do anything hasty." He mustered a grin and shrugged. "No hard feelings, I hope? When I have too much red-eye in me, my mouth tends to get the better of my brain."

Fargo went on, circling the room to come up on the customer at the bar from the rear. He threaded past several tables and was skirting the last one when a heavenly figure in a tight red dress materialized in front of him. Full lips the same color quirked upward, revealing teeth as white as pearls. Fragrant perfume tingled his nose.

"Howdy, handsome," the dove greeted him. "I'm Marcy. Care to treat me to some conversation fluid and chew the cud a spell?" Her warm hand fell on his. "I can make it well worth your while, if you take my meaning."

It had been over a week since Fargo last enjoyed the company of a lovely, willing female. He was strongly tempted. But the knot on the back of his noggin reminded him that he had an account to settle. "Maybe later," he said.

Marcy did not hide her disappointment. "Suit yourself. I just hope I'm still available." She gave his cheek a playful squeeze. "I like gents with broad shoulders and narrow hips. They always have a lot of stamina."

"No one has ever complained about how long I stay in the saddle," Fargo quipped.

"I don't doubt it for a minute." Winking, Marcy sashayed off, her bosom close to bursting at the seams.

Fargo took two more paces and planted himself. He was now less than six feet from the man at the end of the bar, who kept gazing toward the entrance as if expecting someone. Cracking his voice like a whip to be heard above the general din, Fargo called out, "Turn, bastard, and face me."

All talk ceased. Glasses stopped tinkling, poker chips stopped clattering. All eyes turned toward the big man in buckskins.

The beefy customer at the bar had stiffened. Slowly setting down his glass, he pivoted. His features were as flinty as quartz, his eyes as shifty as quicksand. Stubble covered a grimy chin. He wore a flannel shirt and dirty jeans. Strapped around his waist was a long-barreled Remington. "Are you talking to me?" he demanded.

Fargo nodded. "I thought maybe you'd like to try and slug me again, only this time my back won't be turned."

A few patrons commenced whispering among themselves. The man at the counter licked his thick lips, then declared, "I don't know what the hell you're talking about, mister. I never saw you before in my life."

"You're a liar."

All those standing near the beefy man suddenly wanted to be somewhere else. Pushing and shoving, they cleared a wide space around him.

Sullivan, the proprietor, hurried down the bar, waving a dirty cloth in alarm. "See here, fellows!" he said. "I don't know what's going on, but I don't like gunplay in my establishment. Too many bottles get busted. You'll have to take your grudge outdoors."

Fargo had no intention of moving. He waited, poised, for the man at the bar to make his move. "Don't try to deny it was you," he said. "You're wearing the proof."

"I don't know what you're talking about," the man testily insisted.

Without taking his eyes off him, Fargo addressed the barkeep. "Sullivan, did you empty a spittoon out front a couple of minutes ago?"

"Two of them," the proprietor said. "Why?"

"Somebody just jumped me," Fargo explained. "Whoever it was hit me over the head from behind, then ran in here, figuring he could lose himself in the crowd."

More muttering broke out.

Sullivan had stopped shy of the thickset character. "And you're claiming it was Jenkins, here? That's a powerful accusation. What makes you suspect him?"

"He's the only one with tobacco juice all over the lower half of his boots," Fargo replied. He expected Jenkins to go on denying it, to argue the point a while. Instead, the man cursed and made a grab for the Remington. In a blur the pistol flashed up and out, but as quick as Jenkins was, Fargo proved faster. The first blast of the Colt rocked Jenkins on his heels. The second blast smashed him back against the bar where he triggered two wild shots that gouged into the ceiling. Fargo's third and final shot was smack between the eyes.

Jenkins oozed to the floor like so much limp clay. The Remington thudded at his feet and he wound up falling across it, blank astonishment lining his face. His body twitched briefly and was still.

No one else moved. Gunsmoke curled from the end of the Colt as Fargo advanced to verify the man was dead. He would rather have questioned Jenkins before resorting to his six-shooter, but it couldn't be helped. Leaning an elbow on the bar, he replaced the spent cartridge while watching the other patrons carefully in case Jenkins had friends among them. The talk and card play resumed. Most went on about their business, giving him a wide berth.

Sullivan came over. "Hell's bells, mister. You haven't been in this two-bit rat hole two hours, and look at what you've done! That was some mighty slick shooting, if I do say so my own self."

Fargo had stopped at the saloon earlier to wash the dust of the trail from his dry throat, then gone off to find a bite to eat. It had been on his way back that the man named Jenkins had caught him by surprise. He nudged the body with a toe. "You knew this snake in the grass?"

"No better than I do most of my customers," the Irishman said. "Sure, he came in here a lot since he turned up about two months ago. But he wasn't a talkative gent. All I can tell you is that he had a mean streak a mile wide, and that he rode with Wolf Rollins."

"Who?"

Sullivan leaned over the counter to speak quietly. "It's not a name I want to repeat twice out loud. He has ears everywhere, and he can sling lead as fast as you can, friend, if not faster. I'd stay well clear of him, were I you." The bartender looked both ways before going on. "They say Rollins is from North Carolina. He's a big, tough bruiser who showed up in the Springs shortly after word of Ike McDermott's silver find leaked out."

McDermott. Fargo had overheard a pair of faro players jawing about the prospector during his first visit to the saloon. Curiosity had sparked him to ask a few questions, which Jenkins must have overheard. "Is it true that McDermott struck it rich somewhere in these mountains?"

Sullivan wiped a spot of blood off the counter. "That's the rumor. But so far the only silver old Ike has shown anyone is that incredibly huge piece of ore those two fellow told you about a while ago, and a few smaller ones."

"You saw the big one?"

"With my own peepers," the bartender confirmed. "It must have weighed ten pounds, if it weighed an ounce. Pure silver, clean through. Ike brought it in and plunked it down on the bar, right over there." Sullivan pointed. "He treated everyone to a round, and bragged on how he would soon be the richest man in the country, richer even than John Jacob Astor."

Fargo was skeptical. He'd heard such boasts before. After laboring long and hard to strike it rich, a man would find a few nuggets and let it go to his head. "Was it the drink talking, or do you think he really hit the mother lode?"

Sullivan chuckled. "With old Ike, it's hard to say. He does like to run on at the mouth. Still, I've never seen him drink more than he can handle. And I've never heard of him telling a lie."

It wasn't difficult for Fargo to put two and two together. Word of McDermott's find had spread far and wide, luring those who favored the shady side of the law, men like Wolf Rollins and those who rode with him. Men who would stop at nothing to learn where the prospector had made his strike. "Those faro players told me that McDermott is having a hard time of it," he mentioned.

"So I've heard, but old Ike hasn't been by here in weeks so I don't know if the stories are true," Sullivan said, coming around the end of the bar. Placing his hands on his lips, he clucked like an irate hen. "Will you look at all that blood! And I'll have to clean it up!"

"What stories?" Fargo asked as the proprietor stooped to slip his hands under Jenkins's arms.

Sullivan started dragging the corpse toward a door at the back. "That Wolf Rollins and his wild bunch are making life miserable for McDermott. They won't rest until they find out where he struck the vein." Sullivan grunted and slowed to add, "A week or so ago they jumped him on his way here. He got away but they shot a pack horse of his. A month or so ago, it was an old mongrel he was fond of."

"It sounds as if McDermott could use a helping hand," Fargo remarked, trailing along.

"Maybe so, but you won't find anyone in these parts loco enough to buck Wolf Rollins. He has eight or nine gun-sharks working for him. Curly wolves, the whole outfit." Sullivan took a firmer hold. "They'd as soon shoot anyone who meddled in their business as look at them. Mark my words, mister. If you're thinking what I think you're thinking, you would wind up six feet under."

"Jenkins said the same thing," Fargo said.

"Jenkins was a kitten compared to Wolf Rollins," Sullivan noted, and nodded at the door.

Fargo held it open. After the barkeep and the dead

man had gone on through, he returned to the bar. By rights the McDermott business was none of his affair. He didn't know the man. He had no personal stake in the clash. So the smart thing to do would be to mount up and ride out in the morning. But it galled him, being threatened by one of Rollin's men just because he had asked a few innocent questions. No one ran roughshod over him. Ever.

"A penny for your thoughts, handsome."

The tantalizing aroma of perfume told Fargo who was behind him. Marcy's fingertips delicately stroked his ear before settling on his shoulder and caressing his neck. "Can I treat you to a drink?"

"Do bears like honey?" The brunette brushed against him as she stepped up. "I'm afraid there are two things in this world I can't do without. One is good sipping whiskey."

"And the other?"

Like a horse fancier sizing up a thoroughbred, Marcy ran her eyes up and down his powerful frame. She focused on a point several inches below his belt and said huskily, "If you can't guess, you don't deserve to buy me that drink." Her hand strayed to his chest. "I have high hopes for you, big man. Don't disappoint me."

Fargo's laughter seemed to put many of the other customers more at ease. The hubbub became louder, much as it had been before he shot Jenkins. "I'll do my best," he promised.

Over the course of half an hour, Fargo heard her life story. How she had been raised in Ohio and moved west weeks after marrying a fool who thought the two of them could cross the prairie alone. How Cheyenne Indians had shown him the error of his ways. How she had been traded to whiskey peddlers, who took her to Denver. She had decided to head for San Francisco but somehow or other had wound up in Pagosa Springs and now was scraping together enough money to finish the trip.

Similar tales of woe were commonplace. Fargo had listened to more of them than he could count during his wide-flung travels. It was added proof, if any were needed, that the frontier was no place for greenhorns and amateurs. The wilderness was a harsh mistress. It broke the spirit of those too weak to meet it on its own terms. It crushed those who could not cope. In the wild, only the fittest survived, whether they were deer, buffalo, or humans.

"What about you, big man?" Marcy was saying. "What do you do for a living?"

"Some scouting, some tracking, whatever interests me at the moment," Fargo said, seeing no need to be more specific.

They had moved to a table. Marcy contrived to lean forward so that her ample breasts almost spilled from her dress. "What about now? Why are you in the Springs?"

"I'm just passing through."

"That's all?"

Fargo was about to take a swallow of whiskey. Something in the way she asked made him look at her, but she was smiling sweetly so he thought nothing of it. "I never stay in any one place very long," he said. Finishing his drink, he fished in a pocket for coins to pay the Irishman. At that moment a pair of burly hard cases entered. He knew their kind well. They reminded him of coyotes on the prowl, and he automatically lowered his right hand under the table as they surveyed the room. Side by side they stepped to a table and engaged a skinny card player in conversation.

Marcy had also noticed them. "Oh, no," she declared nervously.

"What's wrong?"

"Those two ride with Wolf Rollins. The one with the scar on his jaw is Bob Hackett. The other man is Fess Webster. They're Southerners. From what I hear tell, they were chased out of every state south of the Mason Dixon for one crime or another before they hooked up with Wolf." She fortified herself with a healthy dose of coffin varnish. "They were good friends with Jenkins. I don't imagine they'll take kindly to him being gunned down."

As if to accent her point, the pair turned toward them. Both glowered at Fargo, then spread out to approach him. Marcy promptly rose and moved back out of harm's way. Fargo, using his left hand, poured another shot and made a point of placing the bottle off to one side so it would not be in the line of fire if he had to unlimber the Colt on the spur of the moment. He faced the two men when they were still a good eight feet away and said firmly, "That's far enough."

Hackett and Webster halted. They traded glances and

the one with the scar began to ease his hand toward his Colt.

"Do that, and Jenkins won't be the only one planted tomorrow," Fargo warned.

In the second silence that gripped the saloon since Fargo's arrival, Bob Hackett rested a scuffed black boot on an empty chair and puffed up his chest. "We ride for Wolf Rollins," he stated, as if the statement alone would make Fargo quake in fear.

"It's a rare hombre who will brag about being close friends with a polecat," Fargo responded. Outwardly, he was the perfect picture of a total calm. Inwardly, he was coiled to draw or strike out or do whatever else the occasion might demand should they come at him.

Webster made a sound reminiscent of a riled rattler. "You've got quite a mouth on you, buckskin. Maybe it's time someone closed it for you, permanent-like."

Fargo's smile was masterful. It mocked them and insulted them at the same time. "Care to try?"

Without another word the pair wheeled and stalked into the night. A collective sigh was let out by half the men in the saloon. Sullivan appeared, shaking his head. "I've never met anyone with the knack you have for making enemies. I'd wager you even tussled with the midwife who delivered you."

Grinning, Fargo paid and looked for Marcy. To his surprise, she was nowhere to be seen. He nodded at the proprietor and left. Not taking any chances, he stepped quickly to the side once he passed through the door and stood in the shadows a while to satisfy himself that no one lay in ambush. Several minutes went by before he headed west down the street.

Fargo figured that the incident was over, that he could retrieve his stallion and go find a nice quiet spot to bed down for the night. But he figured wrong. For as he came abreast of the next building, he heard a telltale swishing sound above him. He tried to duck and jump aside, but it was too late.

A noose dropped down over his head.

SAVAGE
FRONTIER

by Frank Burleson

1854. In the East, tension between North and South pulled the country apart, with a weak President helpless to stop it and Secretary of War Jefferson Davis following his own agenda. But in the West, a different threat arose. A new generation of Apache leaders were taking over, who would no longer talk peace with the White Eyes. Instead they would fight with the courage, daring, and brilliance that was the Apache pride.

First Lieutenant Nathanial Barrington was already a battle-scarred veteran of the Apache Wars. But nothing in his passion-driven life as a man and fighting life as a soldier prepared him for the love that flamed in the shadow of the gathering storm—or for the violence sweeping over the Southwest in the greatest test the U.S. Army ever faced and the hardest choice Barrington ever had to make. . . .

from **SIGNET**

Prices slightly higher in Canada.   (180917—$4.99)

WHISPERS OF THE MOUNTAIN
BY TOM HRON

The Indians of Alaska gave the name Denali to the great sacred mountain they said would protect them from anyone who tried to take the vast wilderness from them. But now white men had come to Denali, looking for the vast lode of gold that legend said was hidden on its heights. A shaman lay dead at the hands of a greed-mad murderer, his wife was captive to this human monster, and his little daughter braved the frozen wasteland to seek help. What she found was lawman Eli Bonnet, who dealt out justice with his gun, and Hannah, a woman as savvy a survivor as any man. Now in the deadly depth of winter, a new hunt began on the treacherous slopes of Denali—not for gold but for the most dangerous game of all. . . .

from SIGNET

Prices slightly higher in Canada.   (0-451-187946—$5.99)

EAGLE
by Don Bendell

Chris Colt didn't believe in the legendary Sasquatch, no matter if witnesses told of a monstrously huge figure who slew victims with hideous strength and vanished like smoke in the air. But now in the wild Sangre de Cristo mountains of Colorado, even Chris Colt, the famed Chief of Scouts, felt a tremor of unease in his trigger finger. The horrifying murderer he was hunting was more brutal than any beast he had ever heard of, and more brilliant than any man he had ever had to best. Colt was facing the ultimate test of his own strength, skill, and savvy against an almost inhuman creature whose lethal lust had turned the vast unspoiled wilderness into an endless killing field. A creature who called himself—Eagle. . . .

from **SIGNET**

PROMISED LAND

Jason Manning

Legendary mountain man Hugh Falconer was not free to choose where to go as he led a wagon train he had saved from slaughter at the hands of a white renegade, a half-breed killer, and a marauding Pawnee war party. Falconer took the people he was sworn to protect, and a woman he could not help wanting, into a secluded valley to survive until spring.

But there was one flaw in his plan that turned this safe haven into a terror trap. A man was there before them ... a man who ruled the valley as his private kingdom ... a mountain man whose prowess matched Falconer's own ... a man with whom Falconer had to strike a devil's bargain to avoid a bloodbath ... or else fight no-holds-barred to the death ... or both. ...

from **SIGNET**